# A GENERATION'S JOURNEY

# A GENERATION'S
# JOURNEY

A. S. Washington & De'Quan Foster

New Jersey

Published 2014 by Brickhouse Publishing.

Inquiries should be addressed to
Brickhouse Publishing
25 Wakeman Avenue
Newark, NJ 07104

WWW.DANGERKIDSUNIVERSE.COM
Email: info@dangerkidsuniverse.com

Cover design, Elizabeth Douglas

ISBN-10: 0985887060
ISBN-13: 9780985887063

10 9 8 7 6 5 4 3 2 1

Printed in the United States of America

A. S. Washington dedicates this book:

*To all the lovers and writers of fantasy, superheroes, and science fiction*

*Especially Eric Cooper...*

De'Quan Foster dedicates this book:

*In Loving Memory*

*of*

*Ava Schwamberger*

*&*

*Jeff Daly, Dan Weir, Jackson Patterson, Mike Taylor, and Kam Kobeissi*

*Thanks for all those amazing summers that provided me with the greatest inspiration of all...*

# PROLOGUE

Her slim fingers traced the words upon the page of the old scroll as she read them to herself. For twenty years she'd glossed over them. Their meaning had long escaped her. It had taken her half that time to learn the truth of the words. The other half was spent trying to decipher the map on the opposite side.

Her burgundy eyes scanned the page from left to right, as her head tilted downward. When she reached the bottom, she read the page again and then again.

The words were etched into her memory, but she wanted to be sure of the pronunciation. A mistake could be catastrophic. At the end of a section, the scroll would remind her of how important precision was. Her brow was wet with a thin sheen of sweat as she strolled in anticipation and fear.

Around her, all manner of fish swam outside the glass walls of the underwater labyrinth. She paid no mind to them, though she could hear the bubbling of their gills. She didn't have the patience to give them notice and only the pattering of her boots was any comfort.

The pearl floor echoed along the long circular hallway that drove her deeper underwater. The candles along the left wall ignited each time she drew near to one. It was the only light that pierced the darkness of the foreign structure.

Drawings on the wall between the candles told the story that she'd read many years ago. It was the story that sparked her interest and forced her heart on the purpose she marched toward now. A lone warrior battled against six in the very labyrinth she occupied; yet it showed no ill effects of the war.

She came to a long corridor, as her circular path ended. As she stepped into the hall, she expected hot fire to light her path. But as she walked deeper into the hall, the darkness seemed to grow. The air grew colder and for a moment she stopped, believing she'd seen someone run across her vision.

Breathing in deeply, she pulled her jet-black hair back, and tied it into a ponytail. Goosebumps covered her skin, and the hairs on her arms stood up as she continued forward.

The corridor seemed to go on forever as she walked blindly down the long hallway. Her nerves began to play with her mind again as she felt warm air on the back of her neck. Turning around quickly, she saw nothing but darkness. When she turned back, she felt hot breath on her face and reached out with her hand. She squeezed her fist tight, but grasped nothing but air.

"*Igni*," she spoke softly in a smooth alto. A bright light burst from the palm of her hand, illuminating the hallway.

She could see the end of it, a hundred yards away. She rushed headlong down the hall, her boots slamming hard against the pearl surface. The sound echoed around her and she felt an ominous feeling wash over her, and did her best to ignore it.

When she came to the end of the hall, it was a dead end. A large wall of pearl blocked the way forward. She held the light from her hand up to the wall and she saw the end of the story. The lone warrior had lost to the six he'd battled. They stood over a tomb in a circle, with the lone warrior in it. Each wore a medallion around their necks with both hands outstretched.

She recognized the once foreign words and opened the scroll. The image on the wall was identical to the scroll. It read *Ehr lyheis Dorigon, lu fae'ln ka d'Atlantis.* Her mouth gaped open and tears rolled down her face. Her breathing grew ragged for a while as she dropped to her knees and pulled open the scroll. She reminded herself that she knew the words by heart. Her eyes landed on the inscription on the wall again.

She spoke them aloud. "Here lies Dorigon, the fallen king of Atlantis." Smiling wide, she took to the scroll and began reciting the words, taking care so that she made no mistakes. Quickly she read, with great confidence.

The wall in front of her began to rise as she reached the midway point of the scroll. A resounding boom echoed through the hallway as the wall stopped rising. A mighty gust of air swept into the hall, carrying a large cloud of dust with it. The woman closed her burgundy eyes and turned her head to the side. She allowed her long black hair to absorb the assault of the dust cloud.

Standing, she gathered herself and marched forward into the room behind the wall. Firelight flickered hot from dozens of candles around the room and she could see the large tomb at the center. Around it were a dozen other tombs, large in their own right, but smaller than the one at the center. The center tomb was elaborate. It was carved in the likeness of its occupant.

As she stood over the tomb, the words flew from her mouth in rapid succession. Her heart pounded in her chest as she breathed hard and fast, her shoulders and chest rising and falling rapidly.

*Snap!*

She heard a lock loosen, and then she heard a voice screaming in anger. The chamber shook with fury and the dust that lined the walls floated away in response.

Faster she read, and faster the top of the tomb slid off from the bottom portion.

There were no more words on the scroll, and she watched as he rose up in a seated position. He turned his head toward her, a mean scowl covering his face. She kneeled as his hands touched the sides of the tomb. His long muscular legs arched over the side of the tomb where she kneeled and she folded her arms across her chest. Her hands caressed her shoulders and she watched, as he stood up tall.

His black hair stood high on his head and traveled the length of his back. Clenching his fists, his bare chest and arm muscles twitched, veins visible as his bulk stretched. His teeth were white as pearl behind his pink flesh.

"*Ka* Dorigon," she said as she bowed her head.

When he spoke it was heavy and harsh. His voice echoed around the chamber like a beating drum. "*Hou aerr shing,*" said Dorigon.

"Sorcea, *shong cervas oombel*," said Sorcea, her head still bowed in reverence. Sorcea made certain to tell Dorigon that she was his humble servant. She feared that he might kill her. She could feel the rage rising inside of him like a great storm.

"*Braaga emm lu Novus Fatum,*" said Dorigon coming to stand over Sorcea, his dark burgundy eyes boring into her own.

"The Danger Kids will be yours."

# SLOW CLOCKS

Chatter filled the room in every corner as students filed into the class. Big smiles lined faces and loving bear hugs were exchanged, as old friends met again. Buzzing laughter rang out into the air and everyone seemed to ask the same question.

"Mirely, how was your summer?" said a skinny brown-skinned boy with glasses.

"It was ok Alex," said Mirely with a forced half-smile, her teeth hardly showing. Her chubby cheeks were rosy as if she were embarrassed. She tried hard to look Alex in the eye, one arm crossed over her chest, caressing the back of her opposite arm.

"That's cool!" said Alex with far more excitement than Mirely's answer required.

Alex had always been that way. He shook people's hands too hard, hugged too tight, and when he greeted his friends, he always acted as if they had just come back from summer vacation.

Mirely was his polar opposite, quiet and unassuming. Even in the company of friends she seemed uncomfortable.

"Are you excited about this year?" asked Alex, still beaming.

"I guess so," said Mirely softly, still clutching her arm.

"Come on," said Alex happily, putting his arm around Mirely's shoulder. "We're graduating this year," he said with a wide grin as he squeezed Mirely tight. He motioned his free hand around the room as if showing off art at an exhibit. "Everyone else is excited."

"I think they're talking about summer Alex," said Mirely hunching her shoulders.

"No way, its eighth grade. Just a few short months from now, and we're off to high school," said Alex, nodding his head up and down.

"Eighth grade, I am here," said a boy with a similar build and complexion to Alex, as he walked into the room. His eyeglasses were propped up on his forehead, as he slapped high-fives with friends as he walked past.

"Kareem!" said Alex excited as the two slapped hands.

"Yo, eighth grade. One more year and we're out of here," said Kareem beginning to dance.

"Hi Kareem," said Mirely as she waved her hand quickly.

"Hey," said Kareem still dancing. He snapped his fingers above his head and turned around in circles.

Mirely giggled softly as Alex watched with a smile, shaking his head *no*.

"Hey Alex, hey Kareem, hey Mirely," said a short boy with a sandy complexion. His big brown eyes were wide with wonder, as he looked at Alex, who smiled at him affectionately.

"What's up Anthony?" said Alex as he extended his hand for Anthony to shake.

"Oh nothing," said Anthony bashfully, rocking from side to side as he took in a deep breath. He seemed to want to say more, curling his lips in thought. Anthony stuttered twice trying to speak and then just stared at Alex as his legs wobbled slightly. Alex was sure he was ready to sprint away.

"Dude relax," said Kareem, finally finishing his dance.

"Yeah, aren't you excited about 8th grade, we're finally graduating," said Mirely with a forced smile.

Alex and Kareem looked at Mirely with confused expressions. Mirely turned her eyes to the floor when the boys' brows furrowed in her direction. She wasn't excited about eighth grade. She was afraid. Mirely had no idea what to expect.

Anthony twisted his mouth to one side and breathed in. He wanted to say something.

"Dude, just spit it out, it's only Alex," said Kareem rolling his eyes annoyed. "He acts as if you're some kind of celebrity." Kareem whispered the words quietly to Alex, as he looked at Anthony disgruntled.

"Well…ouch!" Anthony started, and then stumbled forward into Mirely, after his head made a loud smacking sound. Mirely rocked back as she caught Anthony in her arms.

"Dweeb alert," said a large boy with bright blonde hair and fabulous blue eyes. He wore a sleeveless shirt that showed off his muscles.

"Are you ok?" said Mirely to Anthony, who was rubbing the back of his head.

"Hey Brick, why don't you get a hobby," said Alex who stepped toward Brick. Alex had to look up, a full head shorter than Brick, who was bearing down on him.

"Hey Elm – oh I mean Dorkwood," said Brick, laughing at his own joke.

"The name's, Elmwood. You should learn it. You'll probably end up working for me one day," said Alex laughing.

"Over my dead body Dorkwood," said Brick laughing again as he balled up his fist. "Come to think about it," he began and then pulled his fist back to his shoulder.

*Clap!*

A hand wrapped around Brick's wrist as he started to punch.

"Whoa," said a boy who was as big as Brick.

Mirely's eyes sparkled when she saw him and she quickly turned her head away. Kareem stood there with pursed lips and balled fists. He was prepared to pounce on Brick at a moment's notice for threatening Alex.

"Dude, you're late for school as usual," said Brick, yanking his arm away. Brick looked him up and down fast.

"Yeah, well, I got things going on," said the boy with a perfect pearly white smile. He brushed his jet-black hair away from his left eye and extended his hand to Alex. "Elmwood, what's happening science buddy," he said winking his eye.

"Nothing much, now that you stopped Brick from acting like Brick, Aaron," said Alex cutting his eye at Brick.

"First day of school, figure everyone needs a pass," said Aaron nodding his head at Anthony. Anthony acknowledged Aaron's nod, but watched Brick from the corner of his eye still fearful of the boy.

"I'll stuff him in a locker by day's end," said Brick, with a sly smile and wink at Anthony.

"Tomorrow, we'll bash some heads," said Aaron wrapping his arm around Brick's neck and ushering him away. Brick laughed hard as Aaron whispered something in his ear.

"Man!" said Kareem furious, squeezing his fists tighter together. "He's begging for me to light him up."

"Let's keep cool tough guy," said Alex. He turned and clapped Anthony on the shoulder and offered Mirely a smile. Mirely smiled back bashfully. Kareem brooded, blowing air from his nostrils, as they walked in the opposite direction of Brick and Aaron.

The sound of a heel echoed across the floor, as it crossed the threshold of the classroom door, just before the bell sounded at 8:45am. All of the students quickly found their seats as the clapping sound of a second heel crossed the threshold. Whispers rushed between the teeth of the 8th grade class and then the door slammed with a resounding boom. Gasps and air being sucked in fast through nostrils ignited. Suddenly there was no sound coming from anyone, and all eyes were on the short woman standing just inside the door.

Her hair was black and cut close to her head, with a slight curl. She wore dark framed glasses and looked through the lenses intently around the room. When it appeared that Brick was going to whisper something to Aaron, she raised her eyebrows.

"I will assure you, that whatever disruptions you got away with in seventh grade," she started saying to Brick and then looked at everyone again, "will not happen here!" she said emphatically. Her voiced was high pitched, but full and commanding.

Brick cringed at the side of Aaron's head, trying to get his attention and then quickly faced forward. Aaron kept his eyes pressed on the small woman.

Marching toward the blackboard, she picked up a piece of chalk and wrote *Ms. Clark* on the board. She turned around swiftly and locked eyes with Brick, Aaron, and finally Kareem.

"I expect that by now you can all read, but if not, I am Ms. Clark," said Ms. Clark. She smiled softly, wrinkling the smooth caramel skin around her cheeks. "That smile may be the first of many or one of few. The frequency of them from here on out is entirely up to which side of my temper you find yourself on."

Alex and Kareem looked at one another with wide yes. Kareem shrugged as if he didn't care while Alex tightened his interlocked fingers.

Mirely wore a look of dread on her face, while Anthony appeared to be lost in space, looking around at the ceiling above him.

"With that said, it is my job to see that you are successful in scoring satisfactorily on state wide exams, and passing the subject matter in these giant books on my desk," said Ms. Clark of the five books stacked at the center of her desk. "In addition to those, I will require other readings and assignments that will enhance your learning experience."

"Here it comes," said Kareem quietly to himself, but loud enough for Alex and Mirely to hear.

"Shhh…" said Mirely in fear, her eyes facing her desk. She feigned a sneeze and then gasped as she shook her head.

"Bless you child," said Ms. Clark softly.

"Thank you," said Mirely quickly, still visibly flustered, even by Ms. Clark's kindness.

"Now," said Ms. Clark elongating the word. "Each of you will select three books from the shelf behind you by the end of the day. I will record your selections. You will write a ten page report on each by the end of the month," said Ms. Clark with a devious smile as the weight of the assignments registered on everyone's face.

"Count me among the unlucky," said Kareem voicing his disdain with a grunt.

"We'll work together," said Alex trying to cheer Kareem up.

"How about, you do them for me," said Kareem rolling his eyes at Alex.

"Does anyone have any questions?" asked Ms. Clark to the group as silence fell over the room.

"Did they get rid of the slow clocks yet?" asked Kareem with his hand held high.

"What slow clocks?" asked Ms. Clark.

"Well, it has occurred to me that whenever it's almost time to go home, all of the clocks seem to stop working properly. I think it'd be a good idea if the school got rid of them. That way we'll get home on time," said Kareem with a smile as most of the class burst into laughter.

Ms. Clark smiled wide. Both rows of her perfectly straight teeth were visible for the entire world to see. She placed her small hands on her tiny waist and nodded. Her lips curled in a way that seemed to signal her approval of Kareem's good humor, as her teeth disappeared behind her lips.

"Mr. Grant, I can assure you of three things," said Ms. Clark. The class grew silent again as the stoic expression returned to Ms. Clark's face. "One. All of the clocks are in perfect working order. Two. Everyone will be dismissed on time at the end of the day. And three. You will not be dismissed on time because you'll be watching the clock until 3:45pm when detention ends," said Ms. Clark with another big smile.

"Are you kidding me?" said Kareem grabbing the sides of his desk hard, as he leaned over.

"Not in the least," said Ms. Clark with a fierce scowl as she came to stand over Kareem.

He sunk back into his chair slowly and titled his head up slightly to look back at Ms. Clark.

"I-," started Kareem, quickly cut off.

"I'd quit while I'm ahead," said Ms. Clark. She strolled back to her desk and sat down slowly in a big red-cushioned chair. "Answer by saying here," she said as she began to call off the names of the students in her roll book.

The day had nearly drawn to a close as Ms. Clark's class filed back into the classroom. Ms. Clark leaned against the front of her desk as she waited for the students to take their seats. She crossed one leg over the other and folded her arms together.

Anthony stepped into the classroom and shut the door behind him.

"Thank you," said Ms. Clark.

"Welcome," said Anthony with a big smile and a nod of his head.

"Suck up," said Brick, popping Anthony on the back of the head as he walked past. He looked over at Aaron with a smile as the two giggled.

"Looks like you'll have company this afternoon Mr. Grant," said Ms. Clark, eying Brick.

"Same sized brain," said Alex quietly to Mirely.

"Shhh…" said Mirely as she heard Ms. Clark's voice starting to break out over the class.

"Your homework for the night-," said Ms. Clark interrupted by a dozen gasps and then Brick's voice.

"On the first day? Are you serious?" said Brick with a disgusted look on his face.

"Just as serious as I am about your first day of detention," said Ms. Clark.

"This is a joke," said Brick shaking his head *no*.

"I don't joke," said Ms. Clark emphatically.

"Obviously," said Brick, huffing as he rolled his eyes at Ms. Clark.

"I'll obviously be seeing you all week for detention, Bradford Brickens," said Ms. Clark standing up to her full height; one-inch over five-feet.

Brick's mouth flew open as he heard his full name roll off of Ms. Clark's tongue. Brick looked at Aaron who he could hear trying his best to hold back his chuckling. Brick looked at him hard, ready to pounce. Aaron closed his eyes and suppressed his laughter as it swelled inside him. Though his mouth was wide open, no sound came out. Brick did hear a squeak in front of him, and he saw Anthony's body vibrating as he fought back his laughter.

Brick grunted hard inside himself and the muscles in his arms tensed. He slammed his right fist into his left palm and he eyed the back of Anthony's head.

"Tiny brain," said Kareem quietly to Alex, who smiled and fought back his own fit of laughter.

"Quiet," whispered Mirely, not wanting to get into trouble.

"Is there something you'd like to say Bradford," said Ms. Clark. She looked at Brick, and hoped that he understood she wanted no answer. She rolled her eyes and her head in a sarcastic manner, challenging him to say something.

Brick shook his head *no* slowly with a defeated expression on his face. Everyone could see that he was fuming inside. The other students shot quick glances his way. With the exception of Kareem and Aaron, everyone made sure not to lock eyes with Brick.

"Now that the excitement has simmered, allow me to get to your homework," said Ms. Clark cheerfully. Ms. Clark stood up tall and rounded her desk and began to write on the board. The white chalk appeared to swim across the green board in curly cursive handwriting. All it read was *Lost City Festival* in large letters. Under it read the word, *Summary*.

Kareem appeared to be puzzled, staring at the board with his nose flared and lips curled. He shook his head as if to clear it. As he began raising his hand, he felt it snatched down by the wrist. Kareem turned hard to find Alex holding his arm, his eyes wide. Alex shook his head no frantically, hoping to save his friend from Brick's fate.

Kareem snatched his arm away and raised it high, wiggling his fingers.

"Yes Mr. Grant," said Ms. Clark, placing her hands on her hips.

"Crap," said Mirely, turning her eyes away from Ms. Clark.

Kareem turned and gave Mirely a befuddled stare and sucked his teeth as he turned back around.

"I was wondering," said Kareem looking around the room as he felt everyone staring at him. "Why do they call it the Lost City Festival, when the city isn't lost?"

"Good that you asked that question Mr. Grant," said Ms. Clark. Her mood seemed to change as a big smile covered her face. "The Lost City Festival commemorates the last day of labor of the lost city of Atlantis. Legend has it that the city of New Covenant was built directly above the very spot where Atlantis sank many years ago. The festival was just recently revived when a historian dug up some information in a few books he had found."

"So is this Atlantis some underwater city?" asked Alex very interested.

"All that would be left of it now is a ruin," said Ms. Clark somberly. "We're talking about thousands of years."

"You want us to write about some ruined city," said Kareem stunned.

"No," said Ms. Clark in a snappy manner. "I want you to write about what you see at the festival." As she finished her sentence the bell sounded for dismissal.

Chairs screeched across the freshly waxed tile, as wooden chairs with metal legs, slammed against wooden desks with metal legs. Students with seats closest to the door were already halfway down the hall.

Kareem stood and began pulling at his book bag on the floor next to his chair. When he lifted the strap just over his shoulder, Ms. Clark was standing in front of him. He was nearly a full foot taller than her, but she made him feel small. Her hazel brown eyes were stark and piercing. Kareem felt himself shuddering and then fear flooded his senses. Ms. Clark's index finger was pointing directly at the tip of his nose. She then snapped her wrist downward and Kareem's body shot into his seat, almost as if by command.

To his left, Kareem could hear sniggering and turned in that direction. He saw Brick leaning back in his chair with his arms crossed laughing at him. Kareem balled up both of his fists and curled his bottom lip into his mouth, biting it.

As Ms. Clark moved back toward her desk, Kareem could hear Brick whisper, "Whenever you're ready punk."

# FESTIVE

The video game magazine resting between his fingers was supposed to be a distraction. The neatly drawn characters on its pages were supposed to draw him in. He was supposed to be lost in the narrative of the article's writer. His senses should have retreated from the world. By now, he should have been sucked in. The only thought entering his mind should have been about where he'd get the money to buy a copy of the game. But the deafening shrieks of his mother's screams kept leaping into his ears.

Her stomping seemed to reverberate through the walls of his room. The echoes of her pounding feet were familiar. She'd stomped around their last house nearly every day for two years. He hoped that their new house would be better equipped to handle her marching storms. Ray Rivers quickly found that the walls in their new house would be no aid to him.

Ray heard something shatter, and looked over the magazine at the wooden door to his room. He frowned hard and felt himself growing angry. He wanted to go into his parent's room and put an end to the argument. However, his father hadn't exploded yet. His mother always got the first hour of the conflict to herself.

"Maybe if I jumped out the window and broke my leg, they'd give me some attention for a change," said Ray aloud.

Ray flung the video game magazine across the room. It collided with his closet door and hit the floor as he stood from his bed. He was tall, standing four inches over six feet. He closed the distance between his bed and the closet in four strides. The gaming magazine slid to his right as he pulled the closet door open.

Ray whipped a grey hooded sweater on and zipped it up fast. He turned hard to his left and walked fast toward the door. Grabbing the knob, he finally heard it.

"I don't care Gloria!" screamed Ray's father.

It was the unmistakable growl of his father yelling the same words. The three words his father spoke, sort of became his unofficial moniker. Ray thought it was his father's way of making a mockery of his mother. Gloria would argue hard and his father would dismiss everything she had said in a fleeting moment. The hair on the back of Ray's neck stood up. He could look his father in the eye now without having to look up. Yet, he still feared the grizzly bear of a man he was.

Turning the knob, Ray pulled the light wooden door into his room. Looking to his left, he could see his father, dark as night, standing five inches over six feet. His big hands were set on his hips, as he stood over his mother, with a dismissive look on his face.

"This is exactly why were at this point now, Gary," said Gloria, craning her neck as she locked eyes with Ray's father.

"Another lecture?" said Gary rolling his eyes. "Should I get popcorn?" he said sarcastically.

Ray saw his mother's eyes roll, and her lips purse forward in anger. Her small fists were balled up tight. He knew she wanted to hit his father. Ray didn't understand why she never did.

*Crack!*

Gloria broke a bottle of perfume on the floor in front of Gary's feet. Ray looked over and could see the remains of three other bottles of perfume shattered against the floor.

Ray breathed in deeply and thought that it was ridiculous for her to break her own things. To him, it would have made more sense for her to break his father's things. She was angry with him. He didn't understand what reaction she was going for. His father just kept saying it.

"I don't care," said Gary again. "I bought them for you." Ray rolled his own eyes at his father's expression. He could see that his father's indifference made his mother angrier. There was a smirk on Gary's face as he rolled his eyes. Gary's shoulders shook as he laughed.

Ray breathed hard out of his nose annoyed.

*Click.*

*Snap.*

*Thump.*

Ray closed his eyes hard as the sound of his bedroom door echoed into the hall. With his head titled toward the floor he breathed out fast from his mouth.

Looking to his right, he saw his parents looking at him stunned. Both of their mouths were open, but neither of their thoughts became words. Ray looked at both of them and shook his head softly.

"I'm never getting married," said Ray softly. He turned hard to his right and began to trudge toward the staircase.

Ray could hear the pattering of his mother's bare feet against the hardwood floor.

"Ray," she called out to him.

Ray's feet hit the staircase and he took the steps by two. By the time he hit the bottom, his mother had made her way to the top step.

His hand touched the knob to the front door when she was halfway down the stairs. Ray heard his mother call his name again as he opened the door.

"Where are you going?" said Gloria.

"Out," said Ray without turning around.

"Please be careful," said Gloria. She wanted to stop him, but her legs wouldn't move. Tears welled around her green eyes. She pushed her long blonde hair back and shook it. Gloria made a faint grunting sound as she forced back tears.

Ray could hear the knot in her throat. He knew her eyes were full of tears. But he refused to look at her sandy face. It was too pretty to be mean to. Only his father had learned the skill of denying his mother kindness. He knew if he looked upon his mother, he'd lose his nerve. The hardness in his heart would turn to putty. She wasn't blameless in the relationship with his father. He wasn't naïve enough to think their problems were his father's fault alone. They fell apart together. Both were equally hurtful to one another. Both were equally forgetful of him and his feelings as far as he was concerned.

"Aren't I always," said Ray turning his head toward his shoulder, but not looking over it.

"Yes…" his mother started, "Okay," she stopped, even though she wanted to say more. Gloria stood there holding onto the banister. Her right hand caressed her neck as she fought back tears.

Ray pulled the door closed hard as he stepped out onto the porch. A car sped past as he stepped down onto the first stair, giving him a scare. He frowned at the car as it zoomed past. It was moving too fast for a residential street.

"Whatever," said Ray.

He shook his head fast in the hope that it would clear his mind. He descended the stairs quickly, not looking down. Suddenly he felt the string on one of his shoes get stepped on. His body lurched forward. Ray stuck out his hands to try and steady himself. It was of no use. Something knocked into his knees and he felt himself pitched forward. He landed on something hard that didn't weigh very much. At about the same time he felt his shoestring come free, he heard the voice of a girl scream, as he rolled over what he now knew was someone's back.

*Crunch.*

*Clank.*

*Boom.*

"Uh!" said Ray as his head banged against the metal garbage can he knocked over. He rubbed the side of his head fast, as if he could wipe away the discomfort. He grunted and then looked up to see a girl slapping dirt off of her hands.

"Sorry," said Ray as he pulled his legs off of the girl's back.

"I'm ok," she said as she lifted her head. Her chubby cheeks were nearly beet red with embarrassment. She pushed her black hair back twice, tucking it neatly behind her ears.

"You sure?" said Ray as he stood up and extended both of his hands.

"Yeah, I'm ok. Really," she replied. She placed her hands into Ray's waiting palms. His hands were surprisingly smooth as he wrapped his fingers around her hands.

"I'm Ray, I-," said Ray before he was cut off.

"Mirely," said Mirely, introducing herself. She smiled awkwardly, trying not to make eye contact as Ray pulled her up. "You just moved in yesterday right?"

"Hasn't even really been a full day yet," said Ray, remembering the argument he'd just escaped from.

"I live next door to you. Saw you and your family coming in," said Mirely looking up at Ray. "You must go to the high school there," said Mirely seeing how tall Ray was.

"No," answered Ray with a half smile. "I'm supposed to be in the class of some lady named Ms. Clark, at Hernandez Middle," said Ray looking around nervously, dusting his pants off.

"Oh wow, we're in the same eighth grade class," said Mirely excited.

"Really?" said Ray, taken aback by Mirely's excitement. His eyes went wide, and his eyebrows flew up on his forehead as if to say *okay*.

"Yes, and we actually have homework," said Mirely, knotting the left side of her face into a frown. She had noticed Ray's eyes go wide and looked away. Talking to boys was always a chore. It made her feel more awkward than she already did. Getting her hands to stop moving as she talked took effort. No matter how much she tried, Mirely couldn't stop rolling her neck as her hand twirled as she spoke.

"On the first day?" asked Ray shocked. Half of his shock was from watching her head bob in every direction. Ray thought that she must have a spring in her neck; the way it snapped back into place and then rolled again.

"Well it's only a summary of the festival today at the park. It'd look really good if you came to school tomorrow with the homework done," said Mirely. "Ms. Clark is pretty tough." Mirely's bubbly attitude changed to one of dread. The thought of Ms. Clark alarmed her. "I'm waiting for my cousin. You can come with us if you like," said Mirely, getting excited again.

"Thanks for the offer. But I need to blow off some steam. Maybe I'll meet you there." Ray extended his hand again.

Mirely took Ray's hand and looked up into his face, craning her neck a bit. Her cheeks turned a dark red, as she smiled up at his brown face. She thought he was cute, even though his eyes seemed sad. Then she noticed that she was the only one smiling.

"Okay, well nice to meet you," said Mirely as they shook hands firmly and quickly let go.

Ray turned hard and began walking down the street. Mirely screamed out to him.

"The park is that way," said Mirely pointing behind her in the opposite direction.

"I'll figure it out, thanks," said Ray. He didn't know where he was going, but he didn't want any company. The fall had cooled his attitude some, and Mirely's awkward demeanor was a pleasant change. He figured everyone needed a distraction, and he more than others.

"Okay, see you later," said Mirely.

Ray threw up his hand to say goodbye without turning around. Mirely watched him walk away until he appeared to be as tall as she was. All the while, she was tapping the power button on her cell phone.

She'd turned the screen of her phone on and off several times. There were no missed called like she'd hoped for. Only the icons that represented the apps on her phone were present.

Mirely started to walk slowly in the opposite direction toward the park. The air had begun to cool, though summer wasn't technically over for another eleven or so days. She pulled the black shawl she was wearing over her torso to keep warm. The wind blew again, but this time it blew hard enough be heard. Mirely became a bit frightened and looked up at the sky. She noticed that the clouds had become a tad bit darker. They didn't seem grey enough for rain, but a light drizzle she suspected was on the way.

As she made it a full block, her phone began to vibrate in her hand and a popular song played as her ringtone. Looking at her screen, the name Crystal Sancho flashed under a picture of her cousin. She eyed the brunette in the picture for a moment and rolled her eyes in annoyance. Mirely pressed the button on her screen to answer. Just as she was going to speak, her ear was assaulted with a barrage of words.

"Oh my god Mirely, you have to forgive me, I am like, right down the street. I'm literally by your house. You didn't leave me yet did you… Mirely?" said Crystal. The words flew out of her mouth in rapid succession, yet each one was pronounced carefully. "Don't leave me, I've got like one more stop and I'm there. I swear on the mother of heaven," said Crystal loudly. "What are you wearing?" Crystal paused for a moment to wait for an answer, but as soon as she heard Mirely breathe she said, "Wait no, I want to see it."

"How far are you really?" said Mirely, not buying Crystal's story. She was always late whenever the two were supposed to meet.

"Sweetie I swore to God. I swear, just look," said Crystal pleading.

Mirely turned around and could see the bus in the distance, about a block and a half from her house. She watched as the bus rolled toward the stop a few feet from her house. Mirely saw Crystal shoot out of the bus onto the street with her phone in hand. Crystal's knees buckled, but she caught her balance before falling.

"Where are you?" said Crystal looking up at Mirely's house and only seeing two flowers hanging from a post on the porch.

"Down here," said Mirely, waving her hand at Crystal.

"Huh," said Crystal astonished. "So you were going to leave me."

"I've got homework on it, and you missed the first day of school entirely. You're lucky that I told you," said Mirely, quite bravely.

"I'm coming, just wait, please, I don't want to go alone," said Crystal hanging up.

Mirely could see her running toward her. Crystal's dark brown hair was blowing in the wind. Crystal smiled as she approached Mirely. Her cheeks wore deep dimples and her perfectly set white teeth refused to be hid behind her full pink lips. Mirely thought she was beautiful. There was no denying it. All of the boys gave Crystal their attention. She returned none of it.

"Oh my god honey, you look fab," said Crystal, as she wrapped her slim arms around Mirely's neck. Mirely turned red from the pressure and the flow of air being cut off from her lungs.

"Uh, thanks," said Mirely, coughing. "I love you too."

"Like, where did you get this shawl, it's to die for," said Crystal.

Mirely dismissed the compliment, waving her hand and head around dizzily. She hated how she looked compared to Crystal. According to Mirely, her cousin was the picture of perfection.

"You look way better," said Mirely. "But why do you have that on? It's not a party."

"What?" said Crystal, looking herself over and then turned toward a parked car. She looked at her outfit and rubbed her washboard belly. Her dress was pink and fitting. She wore white shoes with a short heel and a white purse draped across her shoulder. Crystal also wore accessories on her ears and wrists.

"See, way too much," said Mirely in a matter of fact tone.

"It's a festival right," said Crystal admiring her reflection in the car window. "I'm just being festive."

Mirely scoffed and turned around, beginning to walk again. The park was just a block and a half from where they were.

Crystal caught up with Mirely and hooked her right arm around Mirely's left. The two walked side by side at a medium pace and admired the Cathedral Basilica of the Sacred Heart from a distance. It was a French-gothic style monument of epic proportion, and one of the largest in the country.

"Could you imagine what it would be like to live inside of something so big?" asked Crystal, smiling her perfect smile.

"It'd be a dream come true," said Mirely, glossing over the large grey stone façade. She curled her mouth to the side thinking about what it would be like. Being a princess was a dream she'd had since she was small. The cathedral was the closest thing to a castle in all of New Covenant.

"Oh my god, yes," said Crystal happily.

Mirely smiled back at Crystal, chuckling a bit as she knocked her shoulder into Crystal's affectionately.

About five minutes had passed since they began walking. They'd been in the park for less than a minute and were cutting across a short grassy hill. In the distance they could see stands, tables, and all manner of food vendors scattered about the field; which sat on the opposite side of the lake from the cathedral.

At the center of the field, closest to the lake, there was a podium set on top of a stage. Two chairs sat on either side of the podium, and all of the seats were empty.

"There's Ms. Clark," said Mirely to Crystal, seeing her new teacher stadium behind the podium.

"Same school since kindergarten, honey," said Crystal.

"Oh there they are," said Mirely as she heard Alex's voice saying *hey*. She saw his hand waving them over. As Mirely and Crystal approached, they noticed Kareem step behind Alex.

"Some party I don't know about," said Alex looking Crystal up and down.

"Yeah right, a party," said Crystal rolling her eyes and licking out her tongue playfully. She and Alex hugged one another tightly. As they drew away from one another, Crystal's smile disappeared, and she cut her eye at Alex. "Why weren't you chasing stories with me today?"

"We had school," said Alex surprised at her question.

"We're reporters. We have to put the first issue out by Friday Elmwood. Don't disappoint me," said Crystal giving Alex a threatening look.

"You're too cute," said Alex waving his hand playfully at Crystal. Suddenly he felt someone step on the back of his shoe. Looking back, he saw that it was Kareem. "Dude, what are you doing?"

"Hey, hey, don't move, she's still right there," said Kareem peeking around Alex's head.

"Do you want me to ask her out for you," said Alex, pointing back with his thumb.

"No," said Kareem emphatically, elongating the word. His eyes were bulging and he shook his head.

"Hi Kareem," said Crystal, her sweet alto voice, music to Kareem's ears.

"Hey, Crystal," said Kareem, raising his hand with a cringed smile as if to say he was present for class. His hand was back by his side in a split second. He began pinching his legs to try and keep his knees from wobbling. "She's still looking," he mumbled to Alex.

"You're hopeless," said Alex with a smile as he turned toward the podium, hearing a tapping sound on the microphone.

*Swoosh.*

*Crack.*

A bolt of lightning ripped across the sky. All of them looked up as the bolt of light zipped in and out of sight.

"Was it supposed to rain?" said Kareem with a frown.

"Not to my knowledge," said Mirely softly.

*Swoosh.*

*Crack.*

Another bolt of lightning struck across the sky in the exact place as the other had, but traveled slightly further.

"That's weird," said Alex.

"Tell me about it," said Kareem looking just as confused as Alex.

"Oh my god!" said Crystal throwing her hands in the air and darting past Kareem. She screamed as she ran, a big smile painting her face.

"Thank God she's gone," said Kareem holding his chest, just over his heart.

"You know, you're pathetic," said Alex.

"Maybe she likes you too. Ever thought about that?" said Mirely, appearing to be bored.

Kareem twisted his face in disbelief regarding Mirely's statement. He burst out into hearty laughter. "No way, good one Mirely." Mirely didn't laugh, and her expression remained firm. He regarded her again, turning his head to one side and then looked back. Kareem could just barely see Crystal running up the hill toward someone.

*Swoosh.*

*Crack.*

A third bolt of lightning traced the same path in the sky again, going a few feet further than the last. The clouds began to grow a dark-grey rapidly. Alex stuck out his hand, as he looked at the sky confused. He didn't feel a drop of water, and then suddenly the grey clouds turned white almost instantly.

"This is some trippy weather," said Kareem hunching his shoulders and then turning his attention to the podium as Ms. Clark tapped the microphone again.

"Welcome to The Lost City Festival," said Ms. Clark excited. A big smile lined her face as she clapped.

Everyone in the field clapped as Ms. Clark stepped down from the podium. Loud music began to play. Two lines of people dressed in tight body suits emerged from behind the stage. They flipped and waved banners about in their hands. People all over were excited. The stands lit up around the field and the loud voices of presenters and performers began to fly into the night air. A fire burst in the distance to the right of the stage. A large hefty man held up a fist full of hot dogs and threw them onto a grill. Those close to him cheered.

"Well let's get to it," said Alex.

As they began to walk Ms. Clark held up her hand to them and nodded. Alex waved back with a smile, while Kareem rolled his eyes. Mirely's fear rose inside of her and she stepped behind Alex.

*Swoosh.*

*Crack.*

A fourth bolt of lightning ripped across the sky again, louder and further than the others. The crowd of people gathered for the festival gasped in fear of the lightning. Ms. Clark didn't move. She looked suspiciously at the lightning bolt.

Alex watched Ms. Clark intently as Mirely and Kareem moved past him.

"What are you doing?" said Kareem turning around, quickly realizing Alex wasn't next to him.

"One sec," said Alex.

Alex watched Ms. Clark, whose eyes were fixed on the sky. She was standing now with her back facing Alex. Her eyes looked to the sky and then to the cathedral in the distance. She was slowly sidestepping in the direction that Mirely and Cyrstal had come.

*Swoosh.*

*Crack.*

A fifth bolt struck and Ms. Clark's pace quickened. The fifth bolt had nearly struck the top of the cathedral. Ms. Clark looked back for a moment. Alex's eyes caught her and he could see a look of dread on her face. She'd only looked at him for a short moment, making him cringe in fear. By the time Alex regained his composure, Ms. Clark was half way up the hill.

"Where's Ms. Clark going?" said Mirely to Kareem. Kareem was paying Mirely no mind. Kareem's eyes were locked on Alex, who was watching Ms. Clark like a hawk. Kareem marched toward Alex and knocked him on the shoulder. "What, are you into Ms. Clark?" Alex seemed to snap out of hypnosis, shaking his head and finding Kareem directly in front of him.

"What! No," said Alex swinging his arms as if to say *yuck*.

*Swoosh.*

*Crack.*

A sixth bolt of lightning zipped across the sky. A resounding boom echoed across the sky. The last bolt had struck the cathedral and the tolling of a bell began. Alex's head turned hard to his right, and he could see Ms. Clark sprinting around a tree. She disappeared from his sight in a split second as a mass of dark grey clouds rolled over the sky again.

A massive gust of wind swept across the field and then a resounding boom echoed across the sky. Shock, fear, and wonder swept through the crowd on the festival grounds. Dozens of people had their eyes fixed on the sky. The weather kept changing rapidly and some became unnerved enough to began to leave. Others sought cover under the large tents scattered around the field.

"Let's go," said Alex with a look of deep curiosity on his face. Alex began marching in the direction Ms. Clark had gone. Kareem held his hands up in submission and then grabbed Mirely by the arm and pulled her behind him.

"Listen, you're not the first guy that's had a crush on his teacher," said Kareem defeated as he moped behind Alex. Alex only looked back and smirked at him. "I can help you with this."

"We're so gonna fail this assignment," said Mirely holding her arm. She hung her head as Kareem continued to drag her by the arm he was holding.

# FAT CHANCE

The clouds were nearly black. Heavy drops of rain pelted the ground. Thin rivers of water rushed down the cracks of the grey soaked sidewalks. Inside the park, crowds of people scattered, hoping to find cover under tents and trees. There were few buildings apart from the cathedral that could hold more than a handful of people. Nearly everyone at the festival was a victim of the downpour.

Brick seemed to be enjoying the rain slapping against the hood of his jacket. His hands were firmly wrapped around Anthony's collar. Brick towered over Anthony, as he pressed his back into a gate.

Anthony's skateboard was tucked under his right arm. He tried to pry Brick's hands from his collar, but his hand was too wet, and the rain was unforgiving. Each time he tried his hand slipped from Brick's wrist.

"Give it up dweeb," said Brick yanking at Anthony's collar.

"What's your problem?" begged Anthony, still trying to pull Brick's hands from his collar.

"Just give up the skateboard, and this all ends," said Brick.

"Come on man, I just got it," said Anthony,

"Did I ask when you got it? I want it," shot Brick, frowning at Anthony, tightening his grip.

"Please Brick, my mom will kill me," said Anthony, pleading. He slid to his left, hoping to slip away, but Brick yanked him back. The gate clanked as Brick slammed Anthony's back into it again.

"Ugh, come on," said Anthony, wincing as pain shot up his back.

"You got two seconds dweeb," said Brick. His face turned into a mask of anger. Hot air shot out of his nostrils, as his lips formed an ugly kiss. He pulled his right hand up by his head and wiggled his fingers. Lowering his pinky finger, he counted, "One."

Quickly his ring finger followed, and he counted, "Two."

Anthony struggled, wriggling, trying to break Brick's grip again. He swung hard, chopping at Brick's forearm. Laughter. He heard Brick laughing at his efforts to free himself. Brick was laughing so hard that his head rolled back. Even his eyes closed. The sound of his jubilant mockery was deafening.

"Three," said Brick, still chuckling.

"Let me go!" said Anthony shouting at the top of his lungs.

A bolt of lightning cracked the top of the cathedral again. Thunder rolled behind it and Anthony cowered in terror. He then wondered if he should be more afraid of the weather or of the young hulk holding his collar.

"Four."

The young hulk was more trouble than the weather Anthony thought to himself. His soaked clothes would eventually dry and his shoes could be cleaned. A butt whooping would hurt. It'd hurt his pride, but more importantly, it'd hurt his body.

"Five."

"Oh come on," said Anthony. He hoped his words might reach the soft side that Brick didn't seem to have. Maybe they'd garner some unseen mercy that Brick had never offered anyone. But his thoughts quickly trailed off as he dropped to his knees coughing. The first punch wasn't so bad. He saw it coming. It was the second one that really folded him up, coming right after the first. He had even less time to prepare for it. Anthony was sure his guts were going to jump out of his mouth.

"Fork it over," said Brick, standing over Anthony.

"No!" screamed Anthony.

Brick's face was brimming with anger. Anthony's eyes flew open. He was just as shocked as Brick at the courage he was able to muster.

"Get away from me," said Anthony as he reeled back, knocking his head against the gate. "Ugh."

Anthony's shoulders flinched and his head rolled to his left as Brick reached down. The back wheels of his skateboard spun against his ribs, as Brick pulled it from his grasp. Terror gripped him at the thought of what his mother would do if he came home without it. Brick turned and took a step. His mind raced at how he could get the skateboard back. Desperation set in immediately and he reacted.

Anthony's hands shot up and he grabbed the end of the skateboard closest to him. Brick stopped, and titled his head toward his right shoulder. His neck twisted and he looked over his shoulder at Anthony.

*Thwack!*

Anthony's fingers slipped from the skateboard as the air left his mouth. Brick's footprint had to be etched in his stomach. There was no way he could have been kicked harder. His skin was singing the blues and the nausea he felt was the back up dancer.

Panting, Anthony rolled onto his side in agony, clutching his belly.

Brick turned and stood over him.

"Aaron," said Anthony woefully, seeing Aaron approaching between Brick's legs.

"Go head, kick him one more time," said Aaron sarcastically.

With a hearty laugh, Brick lifted his hand for a high five. "Dude." Brick swung and only hit air. He turned hard, reached and found more air, as he felt Aaron rip the skateboard from his hand.

"I said give him a break until tomorrow," said Aaron with authority.

"Who made you king of the hill?" asked Brick shocked. Anger and confusion wrinkled his face as he stepped toward Aaron, bumping chests with him.

"Why don't you pick on someone your own size," said Aaron pushing Brick away. His words were a challenge to Brick. Aaron knew he was the only kid in Hernandez Middle as big as Brick. They'd stuffed dozens of little guys into lockers together. They'd done it the past two school years for kicks. One or two girls were even victims of their game.

Brick nodded as if some intricate plan were forming in his mind. "Looks like my old buddy's gone soft." Brick saluted Aaron and his coy expression turned dark as he pulled his lips into his face.

Aaron raised his chin and his eyes begged Brick to say something. Slowly he remarked, "Me, gone soft? Fat chance. Maybe I like to bully people my own size more." The words rolled off his tongue laced with a deeper meaning. Aaron's statement made Brick snarl.

Brick punched his right fist into his opposite palm, and stuck up both of his thumbs. Aaron nodded his head *yes* in recognition of the gesture.

"Later dweeb saver," said Brick, looking at Aaron disgusted. "And you," he began, motioning toward Anthony, feeling gratified when Anthony flinched. "Your knight in shining armor won't be around all the time."

Brick turned around and stuffed his hands in his pockets and walked down the hill toward a set of basketball courts.

Aaron pulled Anthony up and gave him back his skateboard.

"Thanks," said Anthony whimpering a bit as he pressed the skateboard into his abdomen.

"Yeah don't mention it short change," said Aaron, slapping Anthony on the back softly. A loud roll of thunder echoed across the sky, and the rain rushed toward the ground faster. "Let's get some cover."

Anthony nodded his approval, and the two began walking in the same direction Brick went. As they neared the entrance to the park, a woman knocked into Anthony, sending him stumbling to the ground.

"Ms. Clark," said Aaron softly noticing their teacher sprinting toward the cathedral entrance. Ms. Clark didn't slow down, or stop to apologize. She just kept running.

Just as Aaron stood Anthony up, Aaron felt something knock into him. Anthony's foot kicked the back of his heel and knocked him off balance. "Ah," screamed Aaron as he felt himself collapse. Thump. He felt someone fall on top of him.

"Elmwood?"

"Aaron."

"I'm dying," said Anthony, crushed under the weight of Aaron and Alex.

"Sorry," said Alex, standing and pulling Aaron up with him. The two of them helped Anthony up and proceeded to shake hands.

"Why are the three of you chasing Ms. Clark?" asked Aaron. He saw Mirely and Kareem running out of the entrance to the park, the same way Alex had come.

Alex had planned to give Aaron a short summary of what happened inside the park. Yet, there was no such thing as a short summary when it came to Alex. Whatever idea he might have concocted to be concise evaporated the moment he opened his mouth. Every detail had to be explained. The performers were given their time in the limelight and each lightning bolt was a composition of it's own. Kareem wondered if he could cast a spell on Alex by rolling his eyes and making mindless gestures at him. It didn't work, and he wished he were a girl for the first time. Since he couldn't be her, he found himself jealous of Mirely for the first time in his life.

Mirely was talking to her new neighbor Ray who she'd introduced to all of her friends. They were shocked to find out that he was an eighth grader, since he towered over everyone, including Aaron, who was six feet tall.

Kareem was shocked at how talkative Mirely was. He was sure that she had a huge crush on Aaron, but she wasn't paying him any mind. Even when Alex didn't breathe between sentences, she never missed a moment to infiltrate the conversation with her eyes and stare at Aaron. He welcomed the fact that she was gawking at him now. Yet, he didn't want to relive the events that had recently played out. Even Anthony was sucked into Alex's story, which made Kareem feel like the odd man out.

Finally Kareem asked, "Are we gonna to go inside or what."

Everyone gave him a weird look. His outburst disrupted their conversations. Alex's eyes darted from side to side as his face admitted that he was to blame. They were following Ms. Clark, and she'd been inside for ten minutes while they languished outside.

"Let's go," said Alex, leading the way.

"Yeah, uh, I don't do churches," said Ray looking up and down at the big cathedral.

"We're all going," said Mirely, hopeful that Ray would change his mind.

"The man said he doesn't do churches, keep it moving," said Kareem still annoyed with being ignored. He pressed his hand against Mirely's back and ushered her off. Mirely waved back at Ray as he backed away a few steps and then turned toward the direction of the park.

Aaron and Anthony walked past Ray and followed Mirely and Kareem into Sacred Heart. The heavy door made a resounding boom as it closed behind them. All of them turned in fear, staring at the door.

"Probably just the wind," said Mirely, the thunderstorm still raging outside.

"You're probably right," said Alex as he turned around.

Alex's mouth hung open wide at the marvelous size of the nave. As they exited the vestibule, he could barely see the sanctuary at the end of the aisle. The length of the center aisle was a hundred forty eight feet long. Mighty pillars with decorative carvings supported huge vaults, rising up a hundred feet. Ornate chandeliers hung in between the mighty pillars, lighting the center isle of the nave. Along the two side aisles, well-known tales from the Gospels retold Jesus' life on the windows along the wall.

Halfway down the aisle, each of them was looking, but there was no sign of Ms. Clark. Aaron and Kareem both walked down the two side aisles, hoping to see her. Anthony spun around in awe, obviously not among those looking to find Ms. Clark. His attention was undivided, focused on the massive structure shielding them from the rainstorm.

As they reached the sanctuary at the front of the nave, Kareem and Aaron walked quickly toward the others. Alex stood with his hands on his hips. He was turning about and scratching his head in confusion.

"Maybe she needed to pray," said Kareem looking at Alex, who was still turning and obviously in deep thought.

"I don't get it," said Alex, finally standing still.

"Maybe she got close to Jesus, and he took care of everything for her. She probably slipped out one of the other doors which is why we haven't seen her." said Kareem, pointing toward the figure depicting Jesus' crucifixion.

"Or she's in confession, and that's why we can't find her," said Aaron.

"Ten minutes for a confession?" said Anthony, thinking ten minutes was far too long.

"No, she seemed spooked," said Alex, turning toward the figure of Christ on the cross. He walked closer to the sanctuary, and onto the short staircase before the altar.

"Dude, I don't think you're supposed to be up there," said Aaron watching Alex quizzically.

"Are you trying to get closer to God?" asked Kareem jokingly, laughing to himself. Anthony and Aaron laughed with him, but Mirely appeared dreadful again.

Her eyes rested on Alex and she was rubbing her crossed arms to warm them. The air seemed to be growing colder, Kareem rolling his head back to shield his neck.

*Kaboom!*

Thunder boomed outside and then again and then three more times. "Whoa." Anthony thought he felt the cathedral shake, and he could hear the others gasping, having felt the same tremor.

*Crack!*

*Crack!*

The five of them heard two bolts of lightning crackle across the sky and just behind them, more thunder. The raindrops were louder, beating against the magnificent structure of the cathedral. The sound of footsteps off to their right was pattering. A second set of footsteps sounded off from the left of them. The second set of footsteps was moving faster, banging hard against the marble floor. Aaron raced up the stairs toward the altar and stood with Alex. Anthony quickly followed and then Mirely, dragged by Kareem.

"I think we need to get out of here before we get in trouble," said Aaron looking off to his left. The footsteps were growing louder, though Aaron couldn't tell exactly where they were coming from.

"Too late, hide," said Alex, scurrying behind the altar. The steps were closer; the wide nave began to echo.

They were pinned against one another, rubbing shoulders. Mirely was humming softly, fear rising up inside of her. Anthony was slowly rising on his knees, and the other boys followed. They peeked over the altar and could see a nun talking to a priest at the front of the center aisle.

The priest was standing over the nun, his finger shaking in her face. She cowered before him, her head facing the floor. He grabbed her chin violently and lifted her head, so she could look him in the eye.

The priest's head moved closer to the nun's as he titled her head upward. He was tall, a full foot and a half taller than the nun. The priest's hood-covered head moved closer to the nun's. Kareem cringed, his mouth curling in disgust. It was the look that kids made when they saw their parents kiss. He didn't want to see it, but he kept watching. Anthony muttered something that Kareem couldn't make out.

Alex's eyes were focused on the two clergy members. "Don't they, you know take an oath or something," said Kareem quietly to Alex.

"Quiet," said Aaron in Kareem's ear as they watched.

Mirely's humming grew intense and Alex wrapped his hand around her mouth.

The priest spoke to the nun in a language none of them recognized. "*Wei aerr lu kreissas?*" It most certainly wasn't the sound of Latin they'd expected. Each of them knew what Latin sounded like. The priest's voice was heavy and harsh, packed with authority, and a looming threat. The nun tried to move her head, but he grabbed her by the throat, and pulled her closer.

"The scroll said they would be here," said the nun in a smooth alto. Her voice was filled with fear, but she didn't struggle to set herself free.

"*Shing aerr lyh'ang,*" said the priest. He raised his hand and his palm began to glow.

"No," begged the nun.

"What the…" said Kareem.

By instinct the five of them dropped their heads behind the altar. Aaron punched Kareem on his left shoulder, his eyes warning him to keep quiet. Kareem's eyes went wide as he balled his fists and leaned towards Aaron. His cheeks were puffed up with air and he was ready to explode.

"I'll snap you in half," said Kareem softly to Aaron. Kareem's face was wrinkled in anger.

"Fat chance," said Aaron, smiling all the while.

"Quiet," said Alex as he peeked again over the altar.

"...I speak the truth," they could hear the nun finishing her statement to the priest as they peered back over the altar.

He yelled the first two words at the nun. "*Fih lamm,*" His grip then tightened around her neck, and the nun gurgled, struggling to breathe. His raspy voice then grew dark and cold, just as he turned to face the altar. "*Urr amorvde.*" Slowly the priest raised the nun from the floor and turned her toward the altar. "*Nach,*" he said, and with a smooth flick of his wrist, he flung her into the altar and vanished.

*Doonk!*

The nun slammed hard against the altar and the group of them ducked again. She let out a painful gasp as she crumbled.

Alex couldn't help himself, and peeked his head up.

*Slap!*

He saw her hand resting on top of the altar, clawing as she tried she pulled herself up. The inscription on the altar began to glow. Inside the altar they could hear rotating gears. Howling air entered into the nave and locked air began hissing out of the altar, as it slid forward, pushing the nun back. Alex could see her hand reaching and scratching as she tried to pull herself up faster. Then he heard his friends scream. The sounds of their voices suddenly seemed far away and before he could think about what happened, he was sliding down a hard ramp.

Above him he could see the altar slide back into place. Alex could hear the nun screaming *no* faintly as total darkness crept over his eyes. He could hear thumping below him and the muffled sounds of grunts.

"Crap," said Alex as he saw himself sliding into the pile that was his friends. "Watch out!" he yelled, but it was too late. He slammed into them, and rolled onto his side.

"Get your butt out of my face," said Kareem disgusted, pushing Anthony away from him.

Anthony gulped and rolled onto his side. "Sorry."

Aaron stood up first, and then offered a hand to Mirely. She placed her hand into his softly, and smiled as he helped to lift her up. Kareem kicked Anthony's skateboard toward him and he stopped it with his foot.

"Hello," said Alex loudly. His voice echoed loudly and sounded like it was bouncing off of something.

A sweeping sound crept into the secret chamber they were in and then bright orbs around the walls began to illuminate. The chamber was small, shaped like a square and at the center were six altars. Aside from the orbs of light around the chamber, the walls were ivory and bare. Over each of the altars, were circulars crests with symbols on them, rotating, while suspended in air. Each of the symbols, illuminated with a distinct color. As the crests bobbed there, the altars dropped into the floor and the crests began swirling about the room.

"Is this really happening," said Mirely, as she began to back away and stopped when she felt herself leaning against a cold wall.

"Fat chance," said Aaron, backing into the wall next to Mirely.

The others backed up on instinct, except for Anthony who stood still with his mouth hanging open, his foot stuck on his skateboard. One of the crests shot toward Anthony and bobbed in front of him, and then it began bobbing around him. The crest glowed green and the symbol on it was an hourglass. It raced around him faster and then bobbed in front of him again.

"What is that thing?" said Alex.

"How am I supposed to know?" said Kareem, believing the question was directed at him.

Alex and Kareem both turned their heads hard toward Mirely who was standing to their left, next to Aaron. Her eyes were closed, as she spoke, as if she were trying to run a monster out of her dreams. "This isn't happening, this isn't real." When she finally opened her eyes, she saw the crest touch Anthony's chest. The green glowing light wrapped itself around him, and pulled him off of his skateboard into the air.

"Fazzoms," said Alex aloud. It was the word he made up. A silly play off of the world fathom, which meant to understand, comprehend, or to think through, among other things. He'd learned the word in sixth grade and began saying fazzoms when he couldn't understand something, or when he saw something that blew his mind.

Kareem hated the word. "Can't you do me a favor and not say that when I'm around you. Most of all we might be dying at this very moment. I don't want that to be the last thing I remember." Kareem figured he might as well think of a happy thought. "Marilyn Monroe, Marilyn Monroe, Marilyn Monroe," and then he screamed aloud, "Be with me in heaven."

Another crest zipped toward Aaron and bobbed in front of him.

"You're dead," said Kareem, panting. He then looked up to Anthony who he could barely see through the green light wrapped around him.

"Fat chance," said Aaron, and then he screamed as the yellow light illuminating from the symbol on the crest in front of him that resembled a bolt of lightning took him into the air.

A crest with a water symbol shot toward Mirely and took her, and Kareem watched in horror as she floated up into the air.

Another crest with a symbol resembling a shadow shot from the air, and bobbed in front of Alex. "Now you're dead," said Kareem in a blasé tone, shaking his head and letting out air, completely exasperated. Alex looked at him defeated, his shoulders dropped and then another crest settled in front of Kareem with a fire symbol upon it. They both looked at the crest, and then looked at each other. "Now I'm dead too." Kareem rolled his bottom lip down, and shook his head in a way that suggested he accepted his fate.

All of them were swept into the air and formed a circle. The sixth crest came and bobbed in the center of them. A voice filled the chamber saying, *you have been chosen.* Each of them felt a jolt, and then fell unconscious.

# EVIL, MAD

**K**areem began to stir as he lay flat on his back. Behind his closed eyelids, he could feel a bright light affecting his eyes. Opening his eyes slowly, he squinted at the light's brightness. A swirling sound entered his ears as he saw the light spinning around the room. His head hurt, and his ears were ringing as if something loud had just assaulted them.

As Kareem began to sit up, a dizzying feeling took over him and he felt himself rock to one side. "Whoa." He gurgled his discomfort for a bit and then yawned.

Looking up, he saw the sixth crest suspended in air, tracing a radiant light around the room like an arena strobe. From what Kareem could remember, it hadn't moved since he and his friends were pulled into the air.

As he stood up, he could hear his friends begin to stir and he finally looked for them. To his surprise, they were all dressed in costumes. None of them were wearing the clothes they'd gone to the park wearing.

"We're dead and it's Halloween," he whispered aloud to himself. Kareem closed his eyes hard, wrinkling his eyelids and then opened them.

He'd expected them to some how change back into their normal clothes, but his friends still wore the same costumes, as they too began to stand.

"No," said Kareem as he looked down at his hands and noticed they were covered in red fabric, his fingernails still exposed. He touched his face and noticed that he was wearing a band around his face. It was a mask like the robbers wore in old movies. Kareem looked at himself and saw that he was covered in a red, orange, and yellow costume.

"What the," said Anthony looking at Mirely.

She was wearing a short sky blue dress that exposed her arms with white lining down her sides and at the bottom. What most alarmed him were the lettuce green wings on her back that resembled those of a fairy.

"This is unreal," said Aaron looking at Anthony as the five of them stood in a circle. He'd already noticed his own blue and yellow costume. His collar formed a lightning bolt down his torso, just above his belt line; which was also a bolt of lightning. He could feel the mask covering his face, though his hair was still exposed.

Anthony's costume was very similar to Kareem's and his own, except Anthony's mask covered his entire head. On the sides of his heads, up the back of his arms, and at the sides of his boots; Anthony's costume had fabric that extended to sharp points away from his body like a car wing.

"Why is he the only one that looks normal?" said Mirely shaking as she touched her bare skin, looking at Alex.

"Wait, what?" said Alex looking at all of them with jealousy in his eyes.

Alex had the simplest costume of them all. His was a long black trench coat with a single button at the center of his neck. It parted at the waist, just below his belt line. His pants were black, and covered his black boots. His glasses were tinted like sunglasses, and a black lightning bolt took the place of his frames along the sides of his head.

"Pinch me," said Kareem to Alex, who was standing next to him.

Alex squeezed Kareem's forearm with his thumb and index finger.

"Ouch!" yelled Kareem, giving Alex a threatening look.

"You said pinch you," said Alex giggling.

"Not that hard," said Kareem with his fists balled.

"Why did you ask him to do that?" begged Mirely looking at Kareem confused.

"I wanted to see if this was a dream," said Kareem pointing his index finger to the ceiling, "in which case it wouldn't have hurt. Secondly, I wanted to see if we were dead. I expected us to die when the light took us. Sadly, we're still stuck in this...whatever this is." Kareem groaned looking around the room. He hated their current predicament.

"Then there's always hope," said Anthony, his face invisible behind his mask.

"Good way to look at," said Aaron clapping him on the back.

"Which means we could still die," said Kareem.

"Of what?" asked Anthony.

"Uh...starvation, thirst, suffocation. You choose," said Kareem, one side his face curling as if to say *duh*.

"Before that happens, I think we should figure a way out of here," said Alex hopeful.

"How exactly are we going to do that?" asked Kareem sarcastically.

"I'll get back to you on that one," said Alex with a forced smile.

"That's great," said Aaron throwing up his hands. He then dropped down and took a seat on the floor.

"What is that thing?" said Kareem looking up at the crest hovering in the air.

"Not a clue," said Mirely, a tad bedazzled.

Anthony reached toward it, but it was at least teen feet above his hand. The rest of the group looked at him bemused. They hoped he didn't really think he could grab it from where they were standing. Kareem shook his head with indignation at Anthony.

"Wait," said Mirely, squinting as she looked at the button of Alex's coat. Walking toward him, she reached at his neck and touched the button. It was cool to the touch, but she could feel something radiating inside of it. His button was nearly identical to the crest floating above them.

"That's weird," said Alex, feeling a vibrating sensation around his neck.

"There's yours said Anthony," looking at Kareem, pointing toward the center of his chest.

"Holy crud," said Kareem seeing a crest at the center of his chest, inside of a half-sphere on his costume. There were other half spheres on his costume. There was one on the side of each shoulder, and one on top of each of his knees. They were a dark yellow-orange color.

Mirely's crest was around her neck, hanging from a necklace, while Anthony and Aaron's were at the center of their chests as Kareem's was.

"Guess some other unlucky dope was supposed to get that one," said Kareem in a melancholy tone.

"Can we focus on the problem at hand," said Aaron, from his seat on the floor.

"Which is what again?" begged Kareem in his usual sarcastic manner, looking down at Aaron.

"Getting out of here," said Aaron rolling his eyes. "If you're that scared, I'm sure Mirely will hold your hand through all of this."

Mirely looked at Aaron and half-smiled and then shot a glance toward Kareem who was huffing.

"Let's just start looking for a way out of here," said Alex as he approached one of the walls.

"I'll help," said Anthony with excitement as he trotted toward the wall Alex was touching.

"Whatever," said Kareem, walking to the opposite wall.

Aaron stood up and walked past Mirely to the wall behind her, and she walked in the opposite direction, her wings flapping softly.

"Maybe she can fly," said Kareem seeing her wings flutter out of the corner of his eye. He didn't really believe what he was saying. For some reason he was sure he was dreaming and he'd soon wake up.

"I can't," said Mirely.

"Then why are your wings flapping?" begged Kareem forcefully.

"They're doing it on their own!" bellowed Mirely, in a rare showing of frustration.

"Please," said Alex loudly without turning around, hoping to diffuse the situation. It worked.

Five minutes passed, and they were all standing at the center of the room in a circle. The crest hovering above them hadn't move, but kept flashing it's light in every direction.

"Staring at it isn't going to do anything Alex," said Kareem annoyed.

"We can hope," said Alex.

"I'm hungry," said Anthony uninterested as his stomach growled loudly.

"Starvation is getting ready to set in," said Kareem.

"Mirely I think you should hold his hand now," said Aaron with a smile.

"You-," said Kareem and then suddenly the sound of a latch loosening echoed above them.

Crunch, grind, crunch grind. The sound of sliding stone reverberated above them. A shaft opened in the wall and they all looked up. Nothing, but black and cold air sweeping from the entry to the shaft was there. Then they heard a grunt, and the sound of something sliding down the shaft.

Black shoes appeared at the bottom of the shaft, and then the bottom of a black robe. Soon they could see the two ends of a rope swaying from side to side, wrapped around a woman's waist. Whoever it was didn't hit the floor, and roll to a stop as the youngsters had. The nun's feet touched the floor softly as her entire body slipped from the shaft. From slightly bent legs, she stood up.

The crest suspended in the air hummed as the nun stood up and began to bob and dart back and forth. She looked up, her burgundy eyes wide with amazement.

"Hi," said Alex loud and excited. She was a nun. He was sure she was there to rescue them.

The nun removed her eyes from the crest and looked at Alex, puzzled. Watching him step toward her, she frowned and flinched. Alex stopped his approach and looked at the nun confused, holding up his hands submissively. Alex began to form his lips to speak again and the nun grinded her teeth together in an angry scowl. Her chest began to rise and fall slowly. As she breathed, her breath hissed in and out in disgust.

"*Novus Fatum*," said the nun in Atlantian.

"No debating?" said Kareem, befuddled as he tried to pronounce the words of the foreign language dancing on his eardrum.

"Give me your crests or die," said the nun with in a smooth alto voice.

"Whoa, what, wait," said Aaron frowning his shock.

Mirely slipped behind Aaron, cowering in fear, and holding onto his right arm.

"Aren't you a nun?" asked Kareem baffled by her statement.

"Die," said the nun, pointing her fingers toward him.

A buzzing sound zipped into the room. Bolts of purple energy ripped from the nun's fingers, slamming into Kareem with a loud clapping sound. The blow sent his flying into the wall behind him. He landed with a thud against the floor, holding his chest.

*Zip.*

*Zap.*

*Zing.*

Aaron went flying into the wall, after his shoulder nudged Mirely, breaking her grip on his arm. She stumbled side ways and her wings began to flutter rapidly. An intense expression of dread covered Mirely's face as she watched Aaron fall onto the others.

Behind her, Mirely could hear the boys stirring, groaning and grunting their discomfort. Kareem's voice was muddled, but she could hear him telling everyone to get off. He was at the bottom of the pile, trying to push his friends off of him.

The nun's burgundy eyes were boring into her own as Mirely watched her stare. Mirely shook with fear, her wings fluttering faster than before.

"Be a good girl and give me your crest," said the nun. "Do this and I'll make your deaths painless."

Mirely was flabbergasted, as she stood there fearful, her wings flapping uncontrollably. Nuns were supposed to be nice. They weren't supposed to threaten children. "What have we done?" she begged the nun. Her eyes welled with tears as the nun closed her hand.

Purple energy buzzed around the nun's hands as she stared at Mirely. "I will not wait long." Gritted teeth followed her threat. Then her hands burst open and the buzzing cords of purple energy shot toward Mirely.

Impending doom flooded Mirely's senses and her body tensed. Her eyes closed and her arms shot out in front of her. She felt her lungs fill with air, more than she'd ever taken in before. With her head turned to one side, she screamed aloud violently, her palms facing the nun.

Suddenly she felt herself floating in the air as a bitter cold took over her. The short hairs on her arms stood up and a thin layer of ice covered her forearms. Her hands felt like she had stuffed them in snow and she could feel something shooting out of them.

Kicking her feet, Mirely's fear grew, as she no longer felt the floor beneath her. When she opened her eyes she couldn't see the nun anymore. There was a thick layer of cracked ice between them from the floor to the ceiling. Mirely guessed it was a foot thick.

"Mirely?" said Alex baffled, seeing her hovering in the air, a few feet above the darting crest.

"Ah!" Mirely screamed as her wings stopped clapping and she fell from the air.

"Gotcha," said Aaron, as Mirely fell into his arms, knocking him to the floor.

Kareem pulled Mirely up, and then Anthony helped Aaron up.

"How did you do that?" said Kareem looking at Mirely shocked.

"I don't know, it just happened," said Mirely, beginning to shake uncontrollably, falling into Kareem.

"Whoa," said Kareem, catching Mirely, thinking she had fainted.

Her sobbing was muffled, her mouth pressed into his chest. Mirely breathed hard a few times and then said, "That evil, mad…that evil, mad nun. She wants to kill us!"

"I am," the nun scream on the other side of the wall of ice, "going to kill you!"

The nun's scream made the ice barrier collapse. Pieces of ice fell to the floor, shattering into smaller piece.

The nun leapt from the floor, her outstretched hand reaching for the darting crest. It hummed, and the light swirling about the room, pointed toward the shaft. Just as the nun's finger was going to swipe at it, it shot from her reaching hand, down to the floor, and up the shaft. The shaft closed as the crest shot into it.

"No," the nun bellowed and closed her fist high above her head. "You will all pay."

Turning her head toward the five teens, she shot toward them with her fist in front of her. A purple mass of energy formed like a disc, covering the entire diameter of the room. The kids flinched, and then ducked, as the disc grew closer.

"We're toast," said Kareem, seeing the disc of energy just a few inches from him. But instead of destroying them like he thought, it passed through to them and touched the floor.

The nun uttered, "*Igni.*"

A thunderous boom cracked the floor and a vacuum of energy exploded up from under them.

All of the kids were in the air, blasted up from the shockwave, careening uncontrollably. They burst through the wall, breaking through stone. Suddenly they all felt the open air and saw the park lake, thirty feet below them.

# YEAH WHATEVER

Alex was the last of the boys to rise from the water and look up. The hole on the side of the cathedral was huge. The slender space on the left side of the wall had to be where his leg had gone through. The side of his calf hurt from more than treading water.

He was happy to be alive though. Kareem had counted them among the dead several times. When he hit the wall, Alex was certain his final moments had come.

But he was there and so were Aaron, Kareem, and Anthony. Each of them was rotating their arms and kicking.

"Mirely?" said Alex, realizing she wasn't among them.

He looked around and then at Aaron who jutted his shoulders up. Aaron had no clue and Kareem had no comforting words.

"Maybe she bit the dust," said Kareem sarcastically.

Anthony sniggered. He could hear the comedy in Kareem's voice. Alex was mortified. There was no laughter in his chest. His faced appeared grim. His head scrambled in every direction. As the thought came to his mind, he cursed himself in his head.

Looking up, Alex saw Mirely hovering over them, her wings flapping in the air.

Mirely's eyes were focused on the hole in the cathedral. There was a concentration on her face that only found itself there during a test. Taking a test was the only time Mirely was truly confident.

"Mirely!" screamed Alex. Again he screamed her name, but she didn't turn.

"Get out of the water," said Mirely robotically, without turning her eyes to her friends.

"That's my cue," said Kareem. He began to swim toward the field.

"Wait for me," said Anthony, flailing his arms about, trying to catch up to Kareem.

"Mirely," said Aaron softly. He knew she couldn't hear him. He was confused. He didn't know why she hadn't moved. "What is she doing?" Alex looked at him puzzled and afraid.

Then they saw her. Her hand was half closed as if she were holding a ball in her hand. She was gliding toward Mirely, her jet-black hair flapping behind her. Her burgundy eyes were glowing and her mouth was moving slowly. The nun's hand closed around Mirely's throat and squeezed.

Mirely gasped as she felt herself straining to breathe. Slowly her face began to turn blue and the crest around her neck began dancing against her chest.

"Do something Elmwood!" said Aaron harshly.

"I…" said Alex, completely at a lost for words. His mouth was hanging open. His legs and arms still moved by some unconscious force. His brain was detached from his body. He was going to watch his friend be killed in front of him. There would be nothing he could do about it. No way to stop the inevitable end to her life. Alex hoped there was something he could do, but his body wasn't cooperating with his heart.

The nun's glowing eyes shot toward Aaron and Alex. Mirely's wings began to flap faster and she kicked her legs. She was fighting to free herself, but her efforts were in vain. The nun had control of her faculties. Mirely's breathing was labored and her heartbeat began to slow.

"Let her go!" yelled Aaron, gnashing his teeth in a ferocious stare.

"Give me your crests or she dies," the nun exclaimed.

"Lady, I don't know who you are. But you're going to let my friend go or-," said Aaron.

"Or you'll what boy?

The nun's half balled hand opened. Her fingers were spread wide, and a fast howling wind swept across the park. It pushed the falling rain sideways and beat against the tents and tables on the field. A thin line of water began to rise from the lake. The water stopped at the nun's palm and began to join together. Aaron watched the water and saw that it was turning into a thick, sharp piece of ice.

"Knife," said Aaron softly to himself. She was turning the water to ice and making a knife. The revelation made Aaron feel fear. It was a feeling he wasn't accustomed to.

The nun looked at Aaron with malice and smirked. Slowly she wrapped her fingers around the sharp blade of ice.

"No!" screamed Aaron. He wished he could fly, as he slapped at the water with his arms. His balled fists assaulted the surface of the lake. A sinking feeling touched him as he banged away and writhed in fear for Mirely. He saw the nun raise the knife of ice up by the side of Mirely's neck. "No!" Aaron screamed again, and with his right hand reached toward the nun. He wanted to take the ice-knife from her, but she was too far away.

In his ears Aaron heard what sounded like a heavy baseline in a song. He felt like someone punched him in the stomach and felt something coursing through him. Quickly it went, from his stomach to his armpit and then out of his palm.

The buzzing sound of electricity soared away from him, as he watched a golden bolt of lighting race from his hand.

*Thwack!*

The bolt of lightning struck the nun in the chest, breaking her grip, and sent her crashing against the cathedral. Mirely's body shot backward, tumbling in the air toward the field, sailing over Aaron and Alex's heads.

Alex was still dumbstruck, while Aaron was reaching out as if he could grab Mirely out of the air.

"Kareem!" Aaron screamed at the top of his lungs, watching Kareem stand up.

"Holy…" said Kareem watching Mirely flying through the air. There was nothing he could do. That much Kareem knew.

"Crap," said Anthony, wide mouthed and his feet began to patter. The only thought in his mind was to save Mirely. Anthony's muscles tensed and tensed and then stretched. Never had he moved so fast in his life. His speed was unreal and he didn't sink when his feet hit the lake again. Jets of water shot up from lake with each step and just as Mirely was going to the ground, Anthony caught her and tumbled to a stop. "Whoa."

Mirely gasped softly and her starry eyes snapped out of the stupor the nun had put her in.

"Thanks," said Mirely unsure if it were appropriate, sprawled out over Anthony.

"No sweat," said Anthony proud of himself, struggling under her weight. He was the only guy he knew smaller than Mirely.

"What's wrong with him?" said Kareem as Aaron pulled Alex to the edge of the lake.

"Frozen with fear the dweeb," said Aaron disgusted.

A smacking sound resonated from Alex's left cheek as Kareem's hand collided with it.

"Fazzoms," said Alex as he felt the slap.

"Get a grip," said Aarron as he pulled Alex up by the lapels of his trench coat.

"Take it easy," said Mirely as she landed near them.

"Where's..." Aaron began and then saw Anthony speeding toward them.

"Whoa, whoa, whoa," said Anthony tripping on a rock and careening into a tree. "I'm ok," he said quickly, getting onto his feet.

"I'm still lost. I don't know what's going on," said Kareem looking at Anthony. "You people are doing some weird stuff. Kareem forced himself to believe that he was dreaming.

"Let's just go," said Aaron, shaking his head *no* at Kareem.

Aaron trudged forward through the brush behind them. Anthony followed alongside Kareem, and Mirely walked slowly in front of Alex, pulling him by the hand. She knew he was afraid. But she never thought in a million years that he'd ever be more afraid than her. Alex was usually protecting her.

As they made their way back to the field they could feel the rain slow to a drizzle. The sun was peaking through the whitening clouds. Mirely smiled as the sunlight kissed her face.

Her smile was short lived as she heard the sound of the nun's feet touch down in front of them.

"Hey, this day is weird enough without some psycho nun trying to kill us for Halloween costumes," said Kareem annoyed with the nun.

"I am no nun," said the nun, obviously angry about the assumption Kareem had made.

"Then who are you, and why are you trying to kill us?" asked Aaron stepping up hard.

A crowd had begun to gather around them, thinking it was part of the festival. They all stared, interested in the seemingly planned exchange. There were more than enough people in costumes to believe that they were part of some act.

"I am Sorcea. Servant to the great Dorigon, King of Atlantis and conqueror of Earth," said Sorcea with pride and malice.

"Yeah whatever," said Aaron as he stepped closer and stuck his hand out toward Sorcea. He grunted hard and expected a bolt of lightning to strike her, but nothing happened. He did it twice more and looked at his hand puzzled. The onlookers in the crowd were bewildered, looking at one another. Soon, they all began laughing at him.

"You are all weaklings without knowledge," said Sorcea as she began to laugh.

"Stop laughing at me," said Aaron, and then charged toward Sorcea.
*Thwack!*

She struck him with the back of her hand and sent him flying into a group of onlookers. The crowd began to scatter as Aaron stood. He'd been hit with more force than a small woman like her should have possessed.

Aaron grunted his rage again and ran toward Sorcea.

"I think this is what you meant to do," said Sorcea as she opened her palm. A bolt of lightning struck Aaron in the chest sending him flying into the scattering festival patrons. "And one for you." A bolt of lightning struck Kareem in the chest, sending him sliding against the grass.

A girl screamed at the top of her lungs when Kareem hit the ground. People were scrambling in ever direction looking for cover. Bolts of lightning were rocketing in ever direction as Anthony began running at dizzying speeds from Sorcea's attacks.

Another bolt of lightning missed its mark as Mirely shot into the air. The tree behind her took the blow, a chunk of bark falling from its trunk.

Mirely shot toward Sorcea with her hands outstretched. The water still in the air began attaching to her hands. When they were fully covered in water, she was a few yards from Sorcea.

Five gallons of water shot off of Mirely's hands at Sorcea as she screamed at the top of her lungs.

"Child's play," said Sorcea laughing softly to her self. "*Igni*."

A mass of fire enveloped Sorcea's hand, vaporizing the water.

*Bam.* Sorcea's fist slammed into Mirely's face and sent her flying backward on a frozen rope. *Crack.* Mirely collided with Kareem, and knocked him on his butt.

"Children should not play with fire," said Sorcea as she marched toward Alex who was kneeling, holding his hands over his ears.

"Get out of my head," said Alex to himself.

"Poor little boy," said Sorcea as she pulled Alex up by the fabric on his left shoulder.

"Please leave me alone," said Alex, quaking with fear.

"Ahh," Anthony was screaming, coming towards Sorcea from behind.

"Oopsie," said Sorcea as she sidestepped and stuck her foot out, tripping Anthony.

"Whoa," said Anthony as he went rolling like a tire past Alex and into a tree.

"Last offer," said Sorcea as she grabbed Alex by the sides of his head.

"No," said Alex whimpering.

A limping Aaron screamed for Alex, but Alex couldn't hear him. Aarron was holding his chest in agony, coughing each time, as he called out to Alex.

"Give me your crest," began Sorcea as she pulled Alex's head up to look him in the eye, "and I'll save you for last."

His friends were running toward them. Alex could hear their voices and the pattering of their feet, but they were far away from him. He could sense their pain and their fear for him. But he couldn't get rid of the pain in his head. The voice in his head was ugly and bothersome.

"Leave me alone," screamed Alex and his eyes burst with light.

"Uh," said Sorcea, her eyes blinded.

Alex dropped to his knees, breathing hard, still shaking his head *no.*

Just as Sorcea regained her sight, Alex heard a lovely voice utter two words and Sorcea was gone. His friends were closer and he heard the words again. On the sides of his head, he could feel a great breeze and the screams of his friends. He was soon pulled into a dark tunnel and all he could see was black.

# AQUA MAX

The blackness of the tunnel withered away, turning into streaks of white light. The light moved past them quickly, and they saw blue water. Ocean dwelling creatures swam outside of a glass dome that held the seawater at bay. Occasionally one of the creatures would knock into the dome by accident and then flit away dazed.

The ceiling of the dome was lit with bright circular fixtures. The hard marble floor echoed with every step. Their strides were slow and cautious, filled with an immeasurable fear. Mirely's face was covered with fearful wonder. She imagined that the rest of her friends' faces looked the way her own felt. They were all wide mouthed, as their heads turned slowly in ever direction, taking in the dome.

As they neared the center of the dome, sections of the floor folded out in front of them. The square sections rotated and snapped back into place, revealing six white chairs.

"Are those for us?" asked Anthony loudly.

"Who else would they be for?" replied Kareem in an annoyed tone.

"I'm not sitting there," said Aaron.

Alex kept walking toward the white chairs that sat atop a short singular stalk of marble. The back of the chair was short, and Alex put his hand on it. "Seems ok to me." He pulled at the chair's back, and it turned in a full circle.

"You've found a moment to be brave," said Aaron in a confrontational manner.

Alex turned to look at Aaron, but just shook his head *no*, not wanting to confront him. He did fold under the pressure of the battle that they had fought. Something assailed him and made him feel too afraid to act. Alex was ashamed of himself, but he was too afraid to admit it.

"Give him a break, we're still alive," said Mirely.

Alex sat down in the chair and exhaled. Anthony follow suit and plopped down in the chair next to him, just two feet away.

"My feet hurt," said Kareem and found the chair on Alex's other side. "You're on the right hand of power now Alex," said Kareem smiling wide. Alex returned his smile with a nod of his head.

Mirely shuffled over and sat down next to Kareem. She swung her feet twice as she looked around pursing her lips to both sides of her face. Looking at everyone else, she noticed that she was the only one without a mask or eye covering. Someone must have seen her, recognized her face in the park. Her nerves began to drive her mad, and she folded her hands to stop fidgeting. It worked for a moment, but soon she began twiddling her thumbs.

Mirely had noticed that Aaron hadn't come to sit down and gave him the evil eye. He turned his masked face from her, and looked off into the ocean. "Would you stop being stubborn and park your rear?"

"For what?" begged Aaron.

"Just sit down," said Mirely.

"Or what?" snapped Aaron.

"Or we'll sit you down," said Kareem turning his head around.

As Aaron began to saunter over, Alex heard that voice again, uttering two words. This time he recognized them as English. They said, "Park it," and then Aaron yelled.

They all looked back, and saw Aaron flailing his arms in the air. Around them they could hear swirling air carrying him. The air held him over the chair, and then dropped him in it with a thud as it whisked from under him. Aaron grunted and looked to turn around and the voice spoke again, "face forward," and Aaron's body and head snapped forward as if he were pushed.

"What the..." said Kareem unable to turn.

Behind them, they could all hear the slow measured stride echoing across the white floor. The banging of high heels on marble was familiar. The footsteps grew closer and Aaron could soon hear them best, as they rounded the chair just to his left.

Aaron shifted his eyes to his left, and could only see the contours of a woman's body. The physique was covered in white leather, pressed tightly again her skin. Looking, up he found that her face was covered; though her mask did not cover her short black slightly curled hair.

"This day just keeps getting better," said Kareem looking at the short woman standing in front of them.

"Good evening *Novus Fatum*," said the woman.

"Who?" said Kareem and Aaron at once, looking at one another.

"You, all. You're the *Novus Fatum*, the Danger Kids, and peacekeepers of the planet Earth. I am Mystic," said Mystic clad in white leather. "I never imagined it would be you," she said, her tone somewhat jovial.

Mirely moved her head toward Mystic, looking hard at her. "Us what?"

"My students, the *Novus Fatum*," said Mystic, pulling off her mask.

Alex's mouth was hanging wide open when he saw Ms. Clark standing in front of him. Mirely's eyes were wide with fear and confusion. Kareem was facing the ground shaking his head *no*. The questions began to shoot from their mouths. Confusion erupted among them, and Ms. Clark stood there watching. None of them could answer the questions their friends asked. Ms. Clark finally raised her hand and said; "quiet," and they all fell silent.

"Can you all contain yourselves?" asked Ms. Clark.

Alex nodded his head *yes* and looked at the others and they all nodded slowly in unison.

"What the heck is going on?" said Kareem, screaming at the top of his lungs.

"Ms. Clark, please, what's going on?" said Alex, touching Kareem on the arm. His quiet tone seemed to do the trick. Kareem looked at Alex and began to breathe in and out deeply.

"Is anyone else planning to lose their cool before I begin?" said Ms. Clark looking around at them.

Anthony shook his head no as he bounced up and down in his chair. He was excited, he wanted to hear whatever she would say. Ms. Clark could see the smile on his face under his mask.

"Today you faced an Atlantian woman called Sorcea," said Ms. Clark.

"I thought Atlantis was a lost city," said Mirely.

"Atlantis is lost to the surface, but a few Atlantians still exist. I too am an Atlantian," said Ms. Clark, eying the kids as they looked at one another again. She watched them for a short moment, waiting for a question, but none of them interrupted.

"Many years ago a powerful magician by the name of Mysticgo created the crests and filled them with great power. Atlantis was a great city then, ruled by King Lancetavige and Queen Minerva. They'd had a son, Dorigon, who Mysticgo took a great liking to. He possessed powerful magic, even as a boy, and Mysticgo taught him much of what he knew. When that boy became a man, he begged Mysticgo to teach him more. His power was great, but it was not enough for him and he knew Mysticgo had kept the secrets of his true power from him. Mysticgo would not teach Dorigon more, telling him that he had used up all his power to protect the Earth from dangers that they did not yet know. All that Dorigon thirsted for was power and conquest. He begged his father to force Mysticgo to teach him more. Mysticgo warned the king of his son's obsession. In Dorigon's presence, King Lancetavige ordered Mysticgo to cut himself off from Dorigon and never speak with him again," said Ms. Clark breathing in deeply.

"This is where it hits the fan right," said Kareem, as if he knew how the story would turn out.

"In a way yes," said Ms. Clark.

"In what way?" said Alex, eagerly focused on Ms. Clark.

"Mysticgo knew that Dorigon would be unhappy. He felt the rage and anger inside him and decided to act," said Ms. Clark.

51

"He stripped him of his power?" said Kareem hopeful.

"I wish that were the case," said Ms. Clark, breathing in deeply, affected by the story.

"Oh," said Mirely, her eyes glossed over.

"Mysticgo had not lied. The crests required a great deal of his power and he could not show Dorigon his great power as he had before. He'd spent a great deal of time training six children to be the bearers of the crests. When they were ready, he gave them the crests and made them the peacekeepers of Earth. He told them that it was their duty to protect the Earth from every danger. He must have seen Dorigon's treachery coming, because not long after Mysticgo gave the Danger Kids their crests, Dorigon began his conquest of Earth. Dorigon's first act was the killing of his parents and his ascension to the throne of Atlantis. With the throne of Atlantis his own, he set out against humanity and wiped out a dozen civilizations. The first Danger Kids fought his minions for many years and eventually drove them back to Atlantis," said Ms. Clark.

"So they were defeated?" asked Alex.

"No they weren't defeated, just driven back," said Aaron.

"How do you know, you weren't there?" said Kareem.

"That doesn't even make sense," said Aaron.

"Aaron is right," said Ms. Clark flatly. "The Danger Kids had pushed back Dorigon's forces, but they had not stopped him yet. Dorigon himself rose up against the Danger Kids and fought them in Atlantis. As the battle raged between Dorigon and the Danger Kids, Mysticgo returned to Atlantis. He'd hoped he could convince Dorigon to end the war, but the boy he'd loved was gone. So Mysticgo sank the city and took the Danger Kids to a secret hold under the ocean, called Aqua Max," said Ms. Clark as she watched them look around.

"Did all of the Atlantians drown?" said Anthony happily.

"Some, but not all," said Ms. Clark flatly.

"So what happened next and what does this have to do with us," said Aaron, interested, but bored.

Ms. Clark composed herself and continued.

"Dorigon's great power allowed him to adapt to the under water environment of the ocean. He taught the Atlantians to adapt and rebuilt the parts of the city that were destroyed. Soon, he launched an assault on Earth again. Mysticgo tried again to reason with Dorigon, but again he failed. And the boy that was his student attacked his teacher. They fought for a while, pitting their magic against one another. As the Danger Kids arrived to assist Mysticgo who had been in a very weakened state since the sinking of Atlantis, Dorigon slew him," said Ms. Clark. She heard the kids gasp, disbelief in their voices.

"Can't trust anyone," said Kareem shaking his head.

"Then?" said Alex enthusiastically.

"Then, they fought and the Danger Kids prevailed against Dorigon. They drove him back to Atlantis and defeated Dorigon there. Together, they locked him and his followers in a chamber to sleep for all of eternity," said Ms. Clark.

"So that's it," said Aaron, standing up, and looking at all of his friends. "What the heck does that have to do with us?"

"Everything," said Ms. Clark.

"Then tell us how!" said Aaron standing up aggravated.

"If you shut up, she'll probably be able to," said Kareem.

Aaron plopped back down into his chair and huffed out his frustration.

"When the Danger Kids defeated Dorigon, they watched over the Earth for many years. But whatever dangers Mysticgo spoke of that might threaten Earth never came. They grew old and they took their crests to a secret place. Upon the crests they evoked a great spell. The crests would find those worthy of being peacekeepers of Earth, if ever Dorigon should rise again. The descendants of Mysticgo were tasked with the safe keeping of the crests if the *Novus Fatum* ever had need to return. I have not turned from that task since the day I was born," said Ms. Clark.

"No," said Kareem, elongating the word, and then laughed aloud his disbelief and fear. "Ha, this has got to be complete hogwash right," said Kareem as he stood up looking around for an ally. None of his friends came to his aid. None of them comforted him or agreed with his thought process. They were all floored. The weight of Ms. Clark's words were hanging over them like the knowledge of some ugly deed. Even Aaron wouldn't look at Kareem. "You have got to be kidding me right." Ms. Clark didn't react, and she didn't tell him *no*.

"I believe that Sorcea has found a way to release him and was after your crests," said Sorcea.

"Do you have the other crest?" said Alex.

"No, wasn't it with the rest?" asked Ms. Clark.

"Yes, but it flew away when Sorcea was trying to take them," said Mirely.

"Then we have to find it," said Ms. Clark.

"How? That thing was buzzing and zipping all over the place. It's probably killed someone by now," said Kareem.

"It's looking for one worthy of the crest," said Ms. Clark thinking deeply. "Hopefully it finds the last of you before Sorcea can track it down. Max!" Ms. Clark screamed the name *Max* and the dome began to speak, and a control panel folded out in front of the Danger Kids, behind Ms. Clark.

"Here to serve," said a manly voice computerized voice.

"Max meet the Danger Kids, Danger Kids meet Max," said Ms. Clark. Ms. Clark turned around and began banging into the control panel and the glass walls of the dome began to show the city of New Covenant. Each glass wall showed a different section of the city.

"What can we do?" begged Alex.

"Go home. It's getting late. Your parents will be wondering where you are," said Ms. Clark.

"But we can help," said Alex.

"Leave this to me and Max. Tomorrow I'll see you in class," said Ms. Clark as if giving an order.

"Uh yeah, how are we supposed to leave?" begged Kareem standing up. "Uh, like, under water or hadn't you noticed."

One of the glass walls turned white and Ms. Clark turned around.

"Think of where you want to go, and through a portal, these words will take you there," said Ms. Clark and waited for a moment. "Got it?"

The kids nodded *yes* and Ms. Clark turned back around and began typing at the control panel again. Alex read the words.

Alex squinted for a bit, and then slowly read the words as he thought they were pronounced.

*Magortis Teleportis.*

# TOO OLD

The sun peaked at the green grass of the park, as thick grey clouds retreated, replaced by thin white ones. The once cool air, grew warm and comforted Crystal as she glided across the park. Little of her attention was paid to the reporters, cameras, and news vans lining the winding park road. The van with the number seven on it was moving way faster than the twenty-five mile per hour speed limit. She wondered if her idol Jessica Duarte was inside, but she wouldn't look to find out. Mirely wasn't around and she hadn't answered her phone.

The first two times she'd called, Crystal figured Mirely was getting back at her for being late. But missing five calls wasn't like her. Like every other teenaged girl, Crystal knew Mirely was never far from her phone.

Crystal stared at her phone and wondered if she would call again. She was tired of hearing Mirely's voicemail message. Her heart was already beating fast with worry. Compounding her stress would be unnerving. However, Mirely was family and it was her duty to call again.

Her finger slid across the screen of her phone and she found her missed call log. Tapping Mirely's name, she watched the list turn into a picture of Mirely sticking out her tongue. Crystal was begging for the picture to become the in-call icons mute, end, and speaker. She'd hear her cousin's voice and get a chance to berate her. The chastisement she'd spew had been planned over the last five minutes. It was perfect and sure to make Mirely regretful and apologetic.

"Ah!" Crystal screamed loudly as Mirely's soft voice said *leave a message.* "I swear I'm going to kill this girl, this is totally inappropriate if she's not dead already." Twice she had to tap the end icon to end the call. Crystal kept tapping her screen in frustration.

As she slipped her phone into her purse, she could see the bus stop in the distance. Mirely's house wasn't far away, but her mother had already told her to get home immediately. Word of the commotion at the park had already begun to circulate.

Crystal quickened her pace toward the bus stop. Her hand cupped the bottom of her purse. She wanted to feel her phone vibrate if Mirely ever called back. The suspense forced her to take noisy breaths.

Leaning into the sign pole, Crystal began to tap her foot swiftly against the pavement. Her aggravation produced a growling noise in her throat.

She couldn't wait until she was old enough to drive. It wasn't enough to be worried about her cousin. Looking up the street for the bus was a constant necessity. When it got to the corner, she had to see it. Seeing it would tell her to prepare her dollar and change. But it wouldn't make the oversized vehicle come any faster. Getting home as soon as possible was just as much a want as a call from her cousin.

Ten minutes passed and her nerves had calmed. With her arms folded across her chest, she watched her feet as she twiddled her toes. She could hear the hissing sound of the bus' brakes at the top of the hill. Turning her eyes, she saw it round the corner and waved her hand to make sure the driver saw her. Crystal knew the driver was supposed to stop at every stop, but she'd been left before. Stepping closer to the curb, she wasn't going to chance it today.

The doors hissed and she stepped on and slipped her money into the receiver. Bypassing the very front of the bus, she took the first empty seat facing forward, halfway down the aisle. As the bus swung into the road, she leaned her head against the large tinted window and looked out of it.

Night had slowly begun to engulf the daylight as the moon shined brighter than the drifting sun. She exhaled, tired from the action in the park. Slowly her head began to bob about. She blinked her eyes rapidly to keep herself awake.

With the bus swaying as it turned a corner, Crystal grabbed hold of a metal pole to steady herself. Around her she could hear other passengers saying *whoa* as she rocked side to side startled. As the driver righted the bus, her back became pressed against the chair.

A loud song echoed into the air and she could hear the buzzing vibration that she felt on her leg. It was her phone; she thought she'd turned it down. Sliding her hand into her bag, she silenced her phone by hitting a button, and swiftly pulled the phone from her purse.

Mirely. The name she'd seen too many times that day. The voice she wanted to hear the most. Crystal whispered a foul word under her breath, as she stared at her cousin's picture. Allowing her phone to go to voicemail would be appropriate payback. She let the ringtone play for a few seconds and then hit the green icon that read *answer*. Taking the call was of paramount importance. She might not get another.

"I'm so sorr-" Mirely was swiftly cut off before her apology could hit Crystal's ear.

"Don't think you're going to get out of it that easy, I've been worried sick. This is unlike you." Crystal began to ramble. In less than a minute she was yelling in Mirely's ear. "...and what if something happened to you?" Crystal was still going on, though Mirely hadn't been able to say anything since she was cut off. Mirely figured she shouldn't try.

The door to her house felt like a gate keeping her out of a castle. There was no way she would walk into her home being chastised by her cousin. Arguing was out of the question; she'd most definitely start crying. Guilt would wash over her, and somehow the events of the day would be her fault. She'd feel like a deserter. She was soft, too soft to be bold, even with family. So she just listened.

"Not to mention, we're girls. We come together, we leave together," said Crystal finally pausing after five full minutes of talking. Mirely didn't answer. "Did you hang up on me?" Crystal looked at her phone and the seconds were still ticking away on her screen, Mirely's face in pristine color. Silence continued and she said *hello* again, afraid that her phone was playing some kind of trick on her.

Whether it was shock, annoyance or a combination of both, Mirely blinked, rolled her head around and then scoffed. "What?" Surprise registered all over her face and then she said; "Of course I didn't hang up. Why would I do that?"

"Do you understand what I mean?" begged Crystal still as loud as before.

Suddenly Mirely heard a bell ringing in her ear and realized it was the stop request bell on a bus. "Seriously." She paused for a moment and shook her head *no* in disbelief. "Are you really on the bus making all of that noise?" She wasn't stunned; Crystal was willing to make a fool of herself anywhere.

"My heart has been racing for more than an hour your since things calmed down here and I couldn't find you," said Crystal as if Mirely was asking a foolish question.

"I'm sorry, can we talk about it tomorrow?" said Mirely pleading. She didn't have the energy to talk; most certainly not to argue.

"Are you safe?"

"I'm standing in front of my house."

"Call me as soon as you wake up."

"You sure?"

"I'll call you as soon as I wake up," said Crystal giving it a second thought. She was never on time for school. Sleep was far more important to her than listening to her teachers when they talked, since she'd passed every class with little effort each year.

"Okay, kisses," said Mirely, puckering her lips and letting them pop so Crystal could hear. Crystal did the same and the two hung up afterwards.

Mirely was happy that Crystal decided to give a lecture rather than inquire of her whereabouts, as was her custom. For some reason, Crystal was never able to act like a reporter with Mirely. Feeling afraid so much never allowed Mirely to believe that others got just as afraid as she did. Sometimes she thought Crystal was too overprotective, but she was happy to know she could count on her.

Slipping her key into the groove of her doorknob, she heard a latch slide and pop before she turned her key. Looking to her right she could see his tall figure, his head hidden under the hood of his sweater. Goosebumps galloped from her neck to her wrists until she felt like she was covered in them. Her face grew hot and she knew her cheeks were flushed red. All she could think about was how cute he was. Aside from a weird look he gave her earlier, he wasn't full of himself and he didn't seem overly confident. He didn't intimidate her like Aaron did.

Ray. She spoke his name a few times in her mind, trying to muster up the courage to speak. That's how it always was with her. A conversation would be had and when the next opportunity presented itself, she'd flake out.

Her mouth didn't want to cooperate with her heart's desire to strike up a conversation. She watched him pull his key out of the knob's hole and twist it. She thought the opportunity had slipped away, but he raised his key up and slid it in another lock.

*Snap!*

Mirely turned her key hard and snatched the door open to her house and allowed it to bang against the frame of the house.

"What the…" said Ray turning and looking to his left. He laughed at himself, embarrassed for ducking low and looking both ways, only to find a girl wearing a tense smile.

Mirely had another hot flash and rubbed her right arm as if by instinct. She turned to face him and then looked way. He eyed her befuddled and craned his neck forward. He mouthed *oh*, before standing up. His eyes still pierced her as if he could cut through her flesh. "What's up, bad night?" Ray pointed to Mirely's door.

"Tired," said Mirely, unable to produce an entire sentence.

"Yeah, there were some weird things going on at that festival," said Ray inclining his head as Mirely began to answer.

"We never got back to it after being by the church," said Mirely truthfully. She wanted to spew every detail, but she didn't have the energy. She wasn't brave enough to tell him the whole truth. He'd probably think she was crazy any way.

"Think you got enough to do the homework?" said Ray, raising his eyebrows waiting for an answer.

"I think so," said Mirely, still flustered but careful enough not to say much more.

"So I guess I'll catch you tomorrow?" said Ray smiling softly at Mirely.

"Yeah," said Mirely pausing, "catch me," she quickly caught herself. "See you tomorrow." She pulled the door closed hard as she darted inside.

Ray whistled as he watched Mirely scurry into her house before her door slammed. He breathed in deeply watching the wooden door for a moment. Shrugging his shoulders, he turned and twisted the key he'd left in the lock and opened his front door.

The faint smell of amber and spaghetti sauce tickled at his nostrils as he stepped across the threshold. The house was dark, but he could hear one of the televisions upstairs.

Closing the door he looked at the staircase. He was expecting one of his parents to be standing there to talk to him. It was relieving to know that neither of them was there.

Walking slowly past the television to the right of the door, he went into the kitchen and grabbed a soda from the fridge. Twisting the cap fast he chugged a quarter of the dark liquid down as he closed the door.

Taking to the staircase, he scaled the stairs by two, not bothering to brace himself on the guardrail. As he reached the landing, his mother slipped from inside of her room, dressed in a nightgown; half hugging the door as one of her feet caressed the threshold. She exhaled hard and shuffled toward Ray. Ray looked off into the air, rolling his eyes, anger parading back into his chest. But she was mom, so his rage remained at bay.

"I'm glad you're home safe," said Gloria as she hugged him.

Ray felt something flat and hard press against his back and he looked at his mother's hands as the space between them widened again. He recognized the green marble colored box, and watched his mother with a smirk as she tried to fight back a smile.

"I found these in a box and figured I should give them to you," said Gloria handing the box to Ray. She smiled as she placed one hand on her hip, and rustled her hair with the other. Anyone could spot the affinity she had for Ray in her eyes. She looked at him with pride and watched intently as he opened the box. That was the smile she was looking for, full of nostalgia.

Ray rolled his eyes at her and then leaned over, kissing his mother on the forehead. "This is thoughtful, but don't you think I'm a little too old for marbles," said Ray trying to fight back the massive cheese-smile he felt tickling at his chin. He wouldn't smile, he had to brood, brood and prove he was made of iron. Smiling wasn't exactly a way of showing his bravado and he forced himself not to cheese.

"Well yeah, but every now and then you might want to roll them around I guess," said Gloria. "They're yours, so if you got rid of them then that's okay, but…" She trailed off, seeing his lips beginning to form words.

"Of course I'm not going to throw them away," said Ray shaking his head at the thought of parting with them. He tried to play the "too old" card, but he remembered how much fun they were.

"Listen I'm sorry for earlier with dad and all. Uh…" Gloria didn't really want to talk about the argument. But she figured it was decent to say something to her son apologetically. "I'll try to do better for you with dad…at least until we get this whole thing sorted out." She grabbed his hand and kissed it softly, squeezing it with both of her small hands. "I'm glad nothing happened to you, the news said there was some disturbance at the park. It's pretty close by. Were you there?" She asked, needing time to find some words.

"Yeah, but I never really got too far inside. This girl I met was with her friends and they didn't even go in.," said Ray seeing his mother become interested at the mention of a girl.

"You met someone already?" said Gloria surprised.

"We kind of bumped into each other. She lives next door. We're in the same class and all, and she told me we had homework. Our teacher's supposedly some head case that doesn't play many games.

I think I got enough info to get it done," said Ray playing with the top of the marble box.

"Oh is she cute?" asked Gloria interested.

"Mom, homework," said Ray cutting his eye at his mother.

"Right, do your homework, we'll talk in the morning over pancakes," said Gloria looking in his eyes, moving her head side to side.

"Yeah," said Ray. His mother kissed him on the cheek and shuffled back into her room.

Most moms liked to pry, but Gloria had never been a mom to. She afforded Ray many freedoms and she knew the arguments with his father unnerved him. She at least made a little effort, where his father made none at all. "Prick," he said aloud at the thought of Gary and opened the door to his room.

As he shut the door to his room, he suddenly felt hot. He dropped the box of marbles onto his bed and turned on his television. He could hear the marbles knocking into one another, but he didn't hear any fall on the floor. Across the room, he went and opened his window. Skipping and sliding, Ray grabbed the closet door and opened it.

Pulling off his hooded sweater, he could hear the calculating, measured voice of Jessica Duarte. He hadn't meant to turn on the news, so he didn't listen too close as he hung up his sweater.

As he closed the door and took a seat on his bed, he paid a slight bit more attention to what Jessica Duarte was saying. Sure, she was pretty like everyone else on television, but she sounded like every other reporter. Her TV voice annoyed him to no end. Grabbing the remote from the stand that his TV sat on, he was going to change the channel until he saw them again. Those kids with the costumes, their faces covered with masks.

"Too soon for Halloween," said Ray aloud with a grin, looking interested. He plopped back down on the bed and felt a cold gust of wind sweep through his room. The marbles began falling off the bed, rolling around his room. "Crap," he said aloud to himself. But he was too focused on the television to pick them up now. "Unreal," he said to himself as he saw a girl with wings flying, shooting water from her hands.

His mind was spinning and he squinted hard, looking at the flying girl. "No way," he said confused and then heard a second gust of wind as it swept through his window. He raced toward the window closed it and turned again to look at the television. Around her neck he could see a small orb.

Closer he moved to the TV to try and see what it was. Then suddenly a marble was in front of him flashing. He closed his eyes hard. He must have been dreaming. Somehow that day he'd bumped his head, maybe when he had fallen on top of Mirely. But he couldn't have bumped it hard enough to see anything now. He promised himself that this wasn't real, and that it wasn't happening. But when he opened his eyes, it was still there.

Light emitted from it and burst opened into his room, illuminating his entire room with a metallic blue light. "No way," said Ray and raced to his bedroom door and locked it. Whatever was about to happen was going to happen to him alone. His mother shouldn't be taken too. He believed in alien body snatchers. He'd watched enough real life science stories to think it was possible. What happened in the park today was proof of that. The world was weird and it was going to happen to him.

When he turned around to find the glowing orb, it was right in front of him. Its light was cast upon him again and moved as if it was performing a cat scan of his body

"Body snatcher," he said aloud with dread and realized he didn't want to be taken. He didn't want the light to carry him away and he worked up the courage to wrap his hand around glowing orb.

The light in his room disappeared and he turned again to the news on his flat screen. There was a close up of the girl with the wings as Jessica Duarte reported a hotline that anyone could call to report a sighting of the costumed fighters. He studied the girl hard, her face unmasked, but cloaked with some kind of sparkling material that didn't allow a total view of her face.

He continued to study her face and rubbed his head shaking his head *no*. When the commercial came on he stood there stunned for a short time and then opened his hand. He could see some design on the marble sized orb in his hand and it was still glowing, but not casting it's light on him.

"Definitely not one of my marbles," said Ray, looking around at the silver marbles on the floor. He didn't want to clean up and he wished they'd find their way into the box.

Suddenly he felt a jolt of energy course through him and felt a cold sensation on the top of his hand. He closed his eyes as his hand tingled and then he heard the clanking of his marbles against one another.

He could feel air buzzing around him and forceful tapping feeling that never touched his skin hitting his hand. Opening his eyes he saw a thin sheet of metal covering his hand, marbles stuck to them and blue light shining out from the creases in his hands.

"Uh," he muttered, twisting his hand and he watched the marbles shoot into the box. He saw another half dozen marbles fly into the box alone. The top of the box floated in the air toward him. It stayed there, and he knew what he wanted to do. He'd been thinking of it.

Opening his hand he watched the orb that wasn't one of his old marbles float onto the box top. When it touched, the box top slid away from him and folded on top of the box, closing in on the other half.

He stared at the box and rubbed his eyes. Ray then slapped himself as hard as he could. It wasn't a dream. His cheek hurt now, and he noticed the metal covering his hand was gone.

Grabbing the box, he slid it under his bed and curled up under his sheets. "Unreal," he said to himself, and tucked his head under the sheet.

He had to just be having a bad night, and he figured things would be better in the morning.

# MEET ME

Kareem knew Alex was trying to leave the house, but he could hear what was going on inside. Alice Elmwood was yelling at Alex Elmwood, and you didn't interrupt her when she did that. Kareem had been on the receiving end of one of her rants, just for saying good morning. This particular morning, he could hear her loud and clear, scolding his friend for not cleaning up his room. Kareem coughed his laughter into his hand and leaned against the porch rail. No way was he going to be heard, or even be the first thing seen when the door finally opened.

Then suddenly, he wondered if the door would ever open. Last time he'd witnessed Alex getting torn a new one, he had to wait nearly two hours before he came out. They were both late for school that day. But as much as he'd hate it, Kareem would walk through a blizzard with Alex.

*Snap!*

The locked slid out of place. This time in less than five minutes, and Kareem watched with a grin as Alex emerged. Alex stood there for a moment with his head cocked to the side, with his lips pursed to one side. He was waiting for whatever Kareem was going to say. It was going to be tasteless, borderline funny, and down right derisive.

"You're the smartest idiot I know, with the filthiest room I've ever seen. If I were your mother, I'd be mad too," said Kareem clapping his hands and laughing at once.

"Good morning," said Alice loudly, in a commanding alto that forced the hairs on Kareem's arms to salute his best friend's mother. Her short wavy hair was dyed platinum blonde. She wasn't a tall woman, but her presence was noticeable and she made Kareem feel small, even though he was five inches taller.

Kareem's eyes nearly popped out of his head as she pushed Alex aside with her chubby arm. He shuffled away from his mother and rolled his eyes in the opposite direction. Kareem's mouth was filled with air, trying to force back the humor trying to burst free.

"Hi," said Kareem, his voice turning into a high-pitched mockery of his deeper tone. He wasn't going to say good morning. He knew better.

Alice rolled her eyes and scoffed at Kareem as she turned to Alex. "That room better be clean before I get home from work," said Alice and then disappeared behind the slammed door of her house.

Kareem watched Alex trudge down the porch stairs as he swung his backpack over his shoulder. Kareem shuffled down the four stairs behind him and wrapped his arm around him. Alex watched Kareem suck in all the air his stomach could hold through his nose.

Alex would wait for it. The boy couldn't fight it, not with the effort of a thousand men. Kareem was happy to laugh at anyone's expense, especially Alex's.

"BAAAHHH!" His breath didn't stink, and Alex wished it did so he'd have a reason to push him away. It'd give him a talking point to shift the conversation. But it smelled like strawberries and milk, covered with minty toothpaste.

Ten seconds was long enough and being pulled down by the throat was enough reason for Alex to finally shrug Kareem off of him. The books in his bag were heavy enough without Kareem's added bulk, as skinny as he was.

"I'll help you with the room," said Kareem as he stepped back toward Alex.

"You said that last time," said Alex rolling his eyes.

"I was there."

"Yeah, just watching and laughing, no thanks."

"I read that book remember," said Kareem snapping his finger.

"Come to think of it, did you do the homework?"

"No, did you?" said Kareem with raised eyebrows.

"Nope," said Alex, half humming and half speaking.

"She should let us slide, since we were like hit with a monsoon yesterday. Plus, that crazy chick tried to kill us," said Kareem shaking his head remembering their ordeal.

"Did you watch the news?" said Alex interested and hoping he had.

"Me, yeah right, watch the news. The day I watch the new is the day the world ends," said Kareem faking a gag reflex.

"We were on it," said Alex stopping and pressing his eyes into Kareem's.

"No way! How did I look?"

"That doesn't matter, do you think anyone recognized us?" begged Alex.

"We all had on masks, we're good," said Kareem as he began to walk.

"I guess you're right. Let's just get to school and see if Ms. Clark gives us a break on the homework and lets us slide."

Mirely stood leaning against her locker, holding the school paper. The headline read, *Kids With Super Powers Battle A Nun by Crystal Sancho*. Seeing herself on the page as the center of attention was startling. Lifting her eyes from the paper, she looked around to see if anyone was staring at her. No one ever did. All of their eyes were glued on the school paper as they wandered toward their classrooms.

Mirely wondered how Crystal was always able to get the news out so fast. She hadn't seen her at the park since she'd run up the hill toward a friend.

Reluctantly, Mirely pulled herself off of her locker and started down the hall. She walked slow, trying not to be knocked over. Hardly anyone was watching where they were going. Crystal's article was very good. Mirely had read it twice before she got to her locker and another three times while standing there. The details of the article were so accurate that one would think Crystal had been apart of the fight herself.

"I guess that's how they do it," said Mirely to herself.

"How they do what?" said Ray who was standing outside of their classroom door.

Mirely was surprised to see him. She raised the school paper and showed it to him.

"That picture's almost as good as the one on the news last night," said Mirely.

"I think she must have sent it to Jessica Duarte herself," said Ray remembering the image he saw on the news last night. "Your necklace," said Ray touching the charm hanging from Mirely's neck. "It's nice."

Mirely's looked down at Ray's fingers as he caressed the charm. When she looked up he was looking into her eyes with purpose. She was waiting for him to say something, but he never did. He just kept looking at her.

By instinct, Mirely grabbed the charm and tucked it behind her shirt, and then pulled her hair behind her ears.

Ray looked at her funny, wondering why she so swiftly grabbed at the charm. He studied her face and half smiled.

Mirely was so enthralled that she thought he was going to kiss her right there. No one had looked at her that long. The reason as to why he was smiling at her didn't register, even if it was only a halfhearted smile. Any girl would have welcomed attention from a guy as cute as Ray.

"Hey Mirely!" Anthony's happy go lucky voice swept into Mirely's ear, saving her from a moment that was beginning to overwhelm her.

A tinge of discomfort crept into Mirely's neck as she whipped her head around fast. Anthony was running down the hall waving his hand.

"Hi Anthony," said Mirely, putting an arm around his shoulder and hugging him when he arrived.

"Big buddy!" said Anthony playfully, raising his arm high and swinging it down hard.

*Clap!*

Ray stuck his hand out just in time to slap-fives with Anthony. Ray raised his hand high as Anthony had and repeated the gesture again. Anthony moaned. Ray's hand was heavy when their palm's collided. Anthony winced in pain as Ray snapped his fingers and pointed at him with his thumb up.

The bell rang and Anthony scurried into class. Ray motioned for Mirely to go in first. She walked to Ms. Clark's desk and placed her homework in the tray on her desk that said homework in red ink written upon a strip of masking tape. Ray followed a half step behind Mirely and slipped his own paper into the tray.

Ms. Clark stood up and offered her hand to Ray, welcoming him to class. She motioned for him to sit in the front row, the last available seat in the class. "Good morning," she said as she walked to the door and grabbed the knob.

"Whoa, we're here, we're here," said Kareem grabbing the door before Ms. Clark could close it.

Kareem and Alex slipped into the room and quickly took their seats.

"Wow the dorks are late," said Brick, sitting in the back of the room.

"Didn't know you could read a clock that wasn't digital," said Alex dismissively as he sat down.

"Thank you boys for that exquisite exchange of words," said Ms. Clark pulling the door shut.

The room quieted and all eyes were on Ms. Clark. She walked coolly over to her desk and lifted the papers from the homework tray. Sifting through them quickly, she noticed that everyone had done the work with the exception of two. She shook her head *no* and rested against her desk, dropping the papers back into the tray.

"Kareem, is there any reason why you didn't submit the required homework assignment this morning?" asked Ms. Clark raising her eyes and placing them on Kareem.

"Well seeing as there were was like, a tragedy at the park, I assumed-," began Kareem, swiftly cut off as Ms. Clark interjected.

"And you Mr. Elmwood," said Ms. Clark turning her attention to Alex.

"As Kareem said, there were a lot of things going on, not to mention the unexplained occurrence and that maniac nun," said Alex, winking his eye at Ms. Clark.

Ms. Clark frowned at Alex. She knew why he was winking, but she never accepted excuses. No matter how justifiable they may have been. "Is there something the matter with your eye Mr. Elmwood?"

"No," said Alex defeated, knowing she hadn't taken the-bate.

"Then the two of you may stay after class today to finish your assignments," said Ms. Clark, standing and circling her desk.

"What!" He did it again. He became exasperated with her for her inability to be flexible. As scary as she was, he couldn't stomach her matter of fact tone and swift justice. Kareem wasn't going to stand for it, but he wasn't going to stand up. The small woman had made him feel short once. "People could have died yesterday."

"But you didn't," said Ms. Clark firing back.

"Kareem's got a point," said Anthony in an unusual show of courage. He was being more sarcastic than tactful.

"Then you can point him to a good starting sentence after school," said Ms. Clark, thinking that would end the matter.

"I've got to support my buddy," said Anthony, tossing something in the air, and catching it with his opposite hand.

Ray looked at him strangely, not quite seeing the object. Anthony did it again and Ray looked harder, seeing a marking on it, glowing faintly.

Mirely grabbed Anthony by the wrist as he caught the object and looked him in the eye feverishly. "What are you doing?" She barked at him in a whisper, firm and quiet at once. Looking out of the corner of her eye she could see Ray staring.

"What has gotten in to you all?" said Ms. Clark, bursting with incredulity. When she surveyed the room, no one said a word. Kareem sat staring with his lips pushed forward, tight, breathing hard. "Funny that our newest student, Mr. Ray Rivers was able to complete and submit his homework, without having been in class the previous day. For generally astute students, I expected more. Unless you were somehow pushed through the first seven grades with high marks."

"Look at the geeks being torn a new one," said Brick, tapping Aaron on the arm.

Aaron shrugged and laughed at Brick's joke to be polite. He didn't find it particularly funny; he only wanted to avoid a confrontation.

"Why don't you be quiet?" said Mirely standing up and turning around to Brick, and then shooting a dirty look at Aaron sharply for laughing.

Brick sat back in his chair with a look of bewilderment on his face.

"Mirely!" said Ms. Clark, her face full of anger.

"When did you get so brave?" said Aaron looking her up and down.

"How about you decide who you want to be friends with?" said Mirely with a scowl.

"I know who my friends are," said Aaron standing up. He didn't like being challenged.

"Then why don't you act like it?" Mirely stepped closer to him.

Aaron felt like she was challenging him to a fight. Her teeth were bared. Tears were welling in her eyes. Everyone could see her anger boiling, and they were shocked. Mirely had never screamed at anyone. Not in all her years at Hernandez Middle. She was supposed to be the quiet one who folded up into a ball and cried. Two tears ran down her cheeks, but she wasn't exactly pouting.

"You're just acting like that because you like me," said Aaron. It was all he could think of it, an honest statement in bad taste. He knew the rules. You weren't supposed to tell a room of twenty-five of your teen-aged peers that the girl who was a goody-two-shoes liked one of the bad boys. Heck, you weren't supposed give up that kind of information at all, no matter the circumstance. The boy a girl liked was sacred business to be kept between friends.

"What a poor excuse for a friend," said Mirely still staring.

"Sit down, both of you," said Ms. Clark harshly and Aaron dropped into his chair.

Ms. Clark's voice didn't have the same effect on Mirely. She felt the energy brush against her back and neck. Spinning around, she looked Ms. Clark sharply in the eye and then stepped forward toward her.

The wind began to howl outside of the window and the half green - half red leaves on the trees began to fly off of their branches. Mirely's lips were closed, but Ms. Clark could hear her teeth grinding. Thunder rolled across the sky and forced Ms. Clark to step closer to Mirely.

Ray stuck his hand in his pocket. That marble that wasn't a marble was vibrating in his pocket. The symbol upon it was warm, and he knew it was glowing. He looked back at Anthony and saw him squeezing one of his fists tight. He turned and eyed the side of Mirely's face. He saw something, but he couldn't make it out. Ms. Clark saw him watching out of the corner of his eye and grabbed Mirely by the wrists. "I think you should go to the restroom and take care of yourself. Wipe your face and take a moment to think." The whisper was soft, but Ray could hear it, his seat right next to Mirely's.

"Well that was brave," said Brick laughing hard, looking to at Mirely impressed as he eyed everyone else.

Aaron watched Mirely drop her head as Ms. Clark held her wrists and she began to cry. From the corner of her eye she looked at him and then turned quickly away. He watched Ms. Clark release her arms and motion toward the door.

Mirely stormed off and pushed through the door forgetting to close it as she turned left. The wind outside slowed to a calming breeze. Ray looked out of the window. And murmured to himself.

No one spoke for the remainder of the day. Ms. Clark taught an English lesson and required everyone to write a five-page handwritten essay on the pitfalls of society. Only Mirely had finished and was still visibly flustered, hours after her confrontation with Aaron. Ms. Clark sat at her desk the entire time, writing in her notepad and only looked up to check periodic instances of noise or chatter. The room would fall silent and she'd return to writing.

Five minutes before the final bell was scheduled to ring, Ms. Clark stood up. "I'll require Alex and Kareem to finish their homework assignment; along with Mirely and Aaron for their disruptive argument; as well as Anthony for playing with a ball in class. These things are not acceptable here and will not be tolerated. You will all meet me in detention in just a few minutes," said Ms. Clark sternly.

Ray counted five of his peers and figured something was going on. Class had barely started when Anthony was throwing around the ball Ms. Clark had referred to. But he guessed it was like the one in his pocket. That, along with Mirely's face and the weather caused his mind to stir. Hadn't Brick been just as much a part of the disruption. Ray thought as much and found it unfair that Brick wouldn't be included in detention.

"I think that kid back there should have detention too," said Ray without raising his hand.

"Thank you for your police work, but I hand out detention here Mr. Rivers," said Ms. Clark annoyed.

"Well then I think you'd be remissed to not include him," said Ray looking back at Brick.

Brick stared hard at him, narrowing his eyes, nodding his head up and down. Ray was challenging him and Brick had something up his sleeve for Ray if he had to sweat it out in detention because of him.

"Mr. Rivers I would suggest that you keep yourself out of this," said Ms. Clark, looking to her desk, gathering her papers together.

As Ms. Clark fiddled with the papers on her desk, Ray stood up tall, all six foot four inches of him. "And I would suggest that you be more consistent in handing out disciplinary actions."

"You're smart. I like smart people. However, what I don't like are highly suggestive people without any authority making demands in my classroom. This you'll soon find out. You may meet me in detention as well."

"Thank you," said Ray, sitting down with a smile on his face.

"You're welcome," said Ms. Clark and slid over to the homework tray. "Uh," she began as she sifted through the papers, saying, "there," when she found the one that said Ray Rivers at the top. Letting the others fall back into the tray, she held it up with one hand at its center. "Seeing as the heading is all wrong, and you weren't in class; and according to your file you're new to the area. Hmm, and since there's no way you knew anyone here in this town. How could you have possibly known about the homework when I didn't tell you? Perhaps you cheated, and I don't like cheaters."

It was like the sound of a zipper as she tore his homework up into small pieces. "Looks like you're going to have to start over. Wouldn't want an F on the first assignment for plagiarizing would you?" Ms. Clark smirked, wanting to smile harder as she basked in the surprised look on his face.

The bell rang and everyone else slipped out of the class as soon as they could. "Finish your assignment for homework," said Ms. Clark as her students filed out of the room.

"Worse than my dad," said Ray under his breath with a faint smile on his face.

When all of the other students were gone, Ms. Clark walked gingerly to the door. Grabbing the knob, she stood up on her toes and breathed in deeply. Snatching at the knob, she released the door and allowed it to slam hard. "Time for detention," she said with a great big smile.

# FORGIVE ME

Quiet enveloped the room as Ms. Clark sat at her desk, turning the pages of an old book. Ray stared at the back of the wordless cover, admiring the tattered hardcover casing. He could only wonder what the book was about. He imagined some old Greek philosophy or the Holy Bible. Ms. Clark didn't seem like the religious type to him. That was the only thing he liked about her so far. Detention would have been worse if he hadn't worked himself into it purposely.

Mirely sat right next to Ray, staring blankly. Ray thought she was looking at Ms. Clark's book too, but he realized she was staring past her at the chalkboard. Her face was still glum and her eyes were still glossy from crying. Rubbing her back would have seemed weird but for some reason he wanted to console her.

When they met, he never guessed she had an angry bone in her body. Too happy, too bubbly, and too shy to ever get mad. Then he remembered his mother and thought that girls were emotional. No matter how big, or how mature, their boiling point was set at two degrees above freezing.

Ray couldn't understand why no one had said anything. He would have spoken, but everyone else was still writing. He'd handed Ms. Clark his essay ten minutes into detention and returned to his chair. Time crawled at a turtle's pace after he sat back down. Only fifteen minutes had gone by, and she planned to keep them there until four-thirty.

What'd he do to occupy himself for another hour escaped him. His parents didn't allow him to have a cell phone because they believed it'd distract from his studies. Reading was something he was never fond of and only did so inside the pages of comic books and video game magazines.

Ms. Clark didn't seem like the kind of teacher who'd let him read a gaming magazine, so he decided it was best not to try and pull out his latest one.

"Guess I'll just twiddle my thumbs," said Ray sarcastically.

Ms. Clark peaked over her book and caught Ray's eye. "Twiddle them quietly," she said with a scowl.

Ray rubbed the back of his neck and turned his head to the left. Looking out the window he thought that there was no way she could have heard him. Sure his seat was in the front row, but at least five feet away from her desk. "Yeah", he'd said in a whisper to himself. He even admitted to himself that it was laced with sarcasm, but he never intended for her to hear it. The fact that she did notice made him smile, but the occurrence was too weird to let pass.

"How did you hear me?" asked Ray.

"Teacher's ears." Ms. Clark pointed at her ear keeping her eyes on the pages of her book.

"I don't buy it," said Ray aloud so everyone could hear him.

"Excuse me," said Ms. Clark in an authoritative tone that all adults used. Hers was the unmistakable version of an adult caregiver who wished they could slap the kid speaking, but knew it was against the policy of the childcare establishment.

"No one hears that well," said Ray in an accusatory tone.

"I do," Ms. Clark replied flatly, expecting the conversation to end.

Ray smiled at Ms. Clark and then turned around to Anthony. "Yo."

Anthony just nodded and started to bounce in his seat, holding his pencil like a five year old holds a chicken drumstick. "Yo." Anthony tried to sound cool, but failed miserably at it.

"Do you know anyone that can hear a whisper?" Ray looked at the space between his desk and Ms. Clarks. "From five feet away?"

"Maybe Superman," said Anthony enthused.

"Ha," said Ray turning back to Ms. Clark. "You don't exactly look like Superman to me Ms. Clark. Way too short."

Aaron began to laugh and feigned a cough to cover it up. He coughed harder as he saw Ms. Clark begin to stand.

Kareem and Alex leaned back in their chairs watching Ms. Clark move like a lion in the brush, stalking her prey. The tattered book was clutched tightly in her hand and she was clinching her teeth. Alex could see her cheek moving each time she bit down.

"Don't test the limits of my patience," said Ms. Clark standing over Ray.

Ray's left cheek turned up as he smiled at her. He looked over at Mirely and inclined his head forward. "Would you forgive me?" Mirely looked at him confused. Standing up, Ray touched Mirely on the shoulder, and without warning, pushed her hard.

As Mirely fell, Ms. Clark's eyes popped wide open in shock. Anger and disbelief replaced the scowl on her face. Her hands flew up. She was stunned as she stumbled back into the desk as the book was snatched from her hand. Ray turned fast and threw the book as hard as he could at the back of the class. Anthony ducked and rolled out of the way and Aaron stood up looking at Ray hard, ready to fight.

"What did you do that for?" Mirely was severely angry and the clouds outside grew dark and rain fell from them fast, hitting the ground.

"I said forgive me," said Ray as he began to back away as Mirely stood.

He could see it clearly now as he stepped back slowly. A gold mist of some dust-like particles dressed the sides of her face. They made her features difficult to see, but he already knew who and what she was. She was the sweet girl that liked the cute boys; the girl that very few people paid attention to. But she was that girl on TV who could fly and shoot water from her hands. When she got mad enough, she could make it rain, or it rained because she was mad. He wasn't quite sure of how the relationship worked. He heard Ms. Clark say her name. It sounded like a warning, but it was too calm not to be caring and parental. Ms. Clark knew. Ms. Clark was aware of what Mirely was.

"You pushed me," said Mirely, her voice full of judgment.

"Listen to Ms. Clark. Stay cool," said Ray putting his hands up in surrender.

A drop of water touched Ray's ear and he turned his head. Water was floating into the classroom like a line of marching ants. As it made it's way to Mirely it formed a ball of water in front of her chest.

"Mirely what are you doing?"Alex barked the question at her loudly as he stood up.

Kareem pulled at his arm and Alex turned hard on him, trying to free himself. Kareem shook his head no. He wanted to see what was going to happen, with his mouth parted in anticipation.

"I thought you were my friend," said Mirely, her mouth growing tighter as her anger rose.

"I am your friend," said Ray still holding his hands up in surrender.

"No, you're just another mean boy." Mirely placed her hands around the ball of water. "And I don't like you very much."

Ray was fearful of what she'd do. He stuck his hand in his pocket and felt around for his marble. Ms. Clark reached for Mirely and grabbed her by the shoulder.

*Boom!*

Three gallon of floating rain drops slammed into Ms. Clark's face, sending her stumbling off to the side. She began to slip, and then suddenly lost her balance.

"Let me go," said Alex, yanking his arm from Kareem. Breaking free, he began walking toward Mirely in a stiff stride full of purpose.

"Ah!" Ms. Clark screamed. Her hands and legs flew in the air.

*Whiff!*

Alex felt a breeze of cold air zip by him, but didn't turn from his course.

"No," said Ray pulling his hand from his pocket as he heard Mirely scream and push her hands forward toward him.

*Swoosh!*

The sound didn't stop swirling around the room, as the water kept trying to penetrate some unseen barrier. Alex's hand was outstretched and he was groaning, trying not to become overwhelmed.

"Mirely stop." Alex was holding on to a desk, leaning forward, one hand still outstretched. "You have got to get a hold of yourself. Please." He begged her again as his arm began to feel tight. "Please!" He yelled, hoping his voice would break her concentration. Alex coughed air out of his mouth hard, feeling Mirely's anger invade his mind. Her rage ensnared him and a splitting line of pain felt like fingernails scratching against the flesh inside of his head. Slowly Alex began to weaken and dropped to one knee.

In her mind she heard her name being called. As the familiar voice slipped into her mind, her rage eased and she snapped back to her senses. "Alex?" said Mirely. "Oh my god!" She raced toward him and grabbed his wrist as his other knee dropped to to the floor. "I'm sorry, I'm so so sorry." She touched at his arms and neck, looking to see if were hurt. Alex had no visible scars and she held a hand against her chest, just over her heart.

The swooshing sound of the water swirled again and then they all heard it splash against the floor.

Kareem looked around puzzled for a moment and then walked toward the classroom door. He looked out of the slim window into the hallway and didn't see anyone coming.

Ray stood there smiling, looking at Ms. Clark as she stared at him, pulling her arms from Anthony who'd caught her.

"You cover a lot of ground pretty fast," said Ray.

Anthony just tucked his lips inside of his mouth feeling good about himself.

Aaron wasn't amused and he wasn't impressed. He pushed Ray hard, challenging him to a fight.

Ray righted himself with ease. "I don't think you want to do that again," he said in a matter of fact tone.

"Sit down!" screamed Ms. Clark. Her voice echoed around the room, bouncing off of the walls and into the kids' ears.

Anthony zipped to his seat.

"Idiot," said Kareem aloud as he cringed from the pain in his ears, walking toward his desk.

"Cat's out the bag now," said Alex as he stood up, helped by Mirely.

Mirely eyed Ms. Clark cautiously as she walked to her seat, holding her ears.

Aaron pointed at Ray with purpose and balled up his fist, threatening. Aaron parked himself in his seat and punched his palm hard. All he wanted to do was hit Ray in the face.

Ray, the only one not affected by Ms. Clarks deafening scream. Somehow he noticed that it was confined to their classroom. The sound wave never made it's way outside or into the hallway.

"Really, I am sorry," said Ray to Mirely, who was looking at him with disdain. She rolled her eyes and turned her head away from him.

Ray hunched his shoulders as if to say whatever and watched Ms. Clark walk toward him. "Would you like to tell me exactly who you people are? And…" pulling the marble from his pocket, "what this is?" Holding it up, he looked around as the other twelve eyes in the room fell upon the object in his hand.

"The sixth crest," said Alex stunned, looking at Kareem.

"That figures," said Ms. Clark, reaching up and grabbing Ray softly by the chin. She turned his head both ways and saw that his ears were covered in a thin hard sheet of metal. "Now we know where it went." Ms. Clark saw them staring with astonishment.

"That means crazy lady Sorcea didn't get it," said Anthony with a big smile.

"No," said Aaron annoyed, folding his arms across his chest as he leaned back in his chair.

"Still waiting for an explanation," said Ray as he felt the thin layer of metal leaving his ears.

"Everyone, gather around," said Ms. Clark, watching them all stand slowly and then walk toward her.

They formed a circle instinctually. "Hold hands," said Ms. Clark taking Alex and Mirely's hand. Mirely saw that she was standing next to Ray. Goosebumps flared on her arms, but she was still angry, casting an evil eye upon him. Ray turned his palm up for her to hold it and smiled at her.

Ms. Clark grunted to interrupt Mirely and Ray's moment. Ray looked down upon her and she smiled at him. Ms. Clark's smile shocked Mirely, making her uneasy. "That was a nice show you put on; really a thing of beauty for all the ages. You've earned yourself, and all those here, detention for the remainder of the calendar year."

"You've gotta be kidding me," said Aaron, speaking the words that formed Kareem's new facial expression.

"Would you do the honors Alex?" asked Ms. Clark.

"*Margortis Teleportis.*"

A humming sound swept through the room and they all teleported in a streak of light.

# TREMBLE

The fixtures upon the walls were unlit. A single candle just behind a pearl throne flickered with fire. None of Dorigon's face could be seen, but Sorcea had heard him stir when she entered the throne room. His dark burgundy eyes cut through the darkness, his gaze fixed upon her. Accusation filled his eyes, and Sorcea was certain he'd soon kill her. Those who had failed him in years past never lived past the day of their failure. At least that was what she'd read. Though she had read many things she didn't believe, the threats Dorigon made did not seem of the idle variety.

"*Dacas lu tepro d'os al*," said Dorigon softly, his raspy voice scratching from his throat.

"*Emmi Ka?*" Sorcea dropped to one knee and bowed her head. She heard Dorigon scoff and shuddered. Lifting her eyes, she saw that his head was turned to the left. He'd shunned her. She looked to her right to see what he was seeing. Focusing her eyes through the darkness, she stared blankly at the blackness of the ocean outside of the glass wall.

As always, Sorcea could hear the creatures outside swimming about. Yet, with only the candlelight burning, she could not focus her own eyes enough to see them. The breathing and echoing calls of great whales gave her pleasure.

"*Heut'im ja Ka de?*" said Dorigon harshly. Sorcea narrowed her eyes at his question.

"*d'Alantis emmi* Ka," she said in a surprised yet cautious tone. She wondered why Dorigon would question what he was king of. He sat upon the throne. Then she thought and wondered why he called the darkness the teacher of them all. The meaning escaped her.

"*Faeir,*" he began, facing forward again, "*Shing ga'ah faei'd shong Ka.*" Anger and ferocity seeped into his tone. He sucked his teeth and scoffed twice. Judgment had been passed down. He'd called her a failure. Worse, he informed her that she had failed her king. According to the law of Atlantis, it had been written that to fail your king was an act of treason.

Sorcea wondered how she could make it up to him. She searched for the words to set his mind at ease. There had to be something she could do to earn his favor, which would further prove her loyalty. But other than the crests, she didn't know what he wanted. Freeing him from his tomb had not garnered her any praise. "Bring me the Danger Kids," he had said. All she had received was an order. Not even a measure of gratitude for allowing him an opportunity to avenge his defeat. When there were no Danger Kids to find, it was the crests he wanted. He paid her back by throwing her into a stone. Death had to be certain and all she could think of now, was how to save herself.

"*Woi ken ja'eb de cervas?*" Sorcea begged Dorigon to tell her how she could serve him. His harsh stare ordered her to plead. "*Tei emm emmi Ka.*" Her tone was bordering on indignation. But even if it was indignant, it was also a plea for mercy. If he could not read it in her tone, he could read it in her welling eyes.

The tension was unbearable as she watched him inhale deeply. She could see the silhouette of his large chest rise. His hands braced the arms of his throne. Sorcea was happy when he let them go just a moment later. Then the comfort she felt drifted when she felt his consciousness brush against her mind. On reflex she closed her mind quickly. Dorigon growled and she gasped with fear.

"*Odu shing ga'ah suma tige ta heish?*" said Dorigon harshly, growling as every word rolled off of his tongue.

"I'm not hiding anything," said Sorcea quickly, responding in English by reflex. She'd chosen her next words wisely in Atlantian, as not to further offend Dorigon. He understood English well enough to speak and understand the language. However, he'd found it disgusting and refused to speak it or have any of his servants speak to him in it. *"Ja sha amorvde ni cervas ta emmi Ka."* Sorcea opened her mind and pushed the images of her memories toward Dorigion's consciousness. She showed him the events in the secret chamber of the cathedral, the fight upon the park grass, and the appearance of a woman she knew well.

*"Osa shing wir italehase?"* asked Dorigon inquisitively, a faint smile upon his face.

Sorcea paused and blinked fast with her head down as the Atlantian words echoed in her head, saying '*Keis Ehya.*' Constantly he repeated them, and she finally looked up at Dorigon. Tears welled in her eyes, but she wouldn't allow them to fall.

Dorigon stood and walked toward her, holding a pearl chalice in his left hand. As he neared Sorcea, the light fixtures around the throne room alit with fire as he said *"Igni."* Sorcea looked up and he touched the botton of her chin, commanding her to stand. She did so slowly. At full height, she turned her eyes to the floor in reverent respect of her king. It was the custom in Atlantis to keep your head bowed in the presence of the king when he was alone with you. To look directly at him was to make a threat upon his life.

*"Preyvo shong filiti e'odu tis tiga,"* said Dorigon in the calmest tone his harsh voice could manage.

*"Ja sha."* Sorcia promised to fulfill his command.

Dorgin leaned into Sorcea and kissed her upon her forehead. For the first time since he'd risen from his tomb, he felt a measure of content. Sorcea could not turn back from his behest. To do so would mean disgrace. His kiss upon her forehead symbolized the favor and trust of the King of Atlantis. When presented with the opportunity, she must fulfill her duty. Only death by the hand of her enemy, or by her own would suffice.

Sorcea bowed again and then turned, walking from the throne room. Her mind was racing. All she could think of was Dorigon's request. What alarmed her was how fast she had agreed to it. Yet, as she thought about it, she knew why. Anger and hatred welled up inside of her as she thought of the past. Her parents never celebrated her, and nothing had been particularly special about her.

"Not until I found this." Reaching behind her black shirt, she pulled at a black gem hanging from a silver necklace. It had been a gift given to her oldest ancestor long ago. Though only a piece of a whole, it gave her far greater power than she'd once had. It was the thing that led her to the scrolls and to where Dorigon slept.

She smiled, remembering how much more it had led her to. They were the things she'd use to carry out Dorigon's orders.

Finding herself standing at one of the glass walls, she peered out of it, looking up. Above her she could see the smallest speckles of the sun's radiant rays. "*Margortis teleportis,*" she murmured and teleported to the surface of the Atlantic Ocean. Her feet touched softly onto the water and she stood upon the waves, her black hair blowing in the gusting wind.

In her mind she saw the faces of the new Danger Kids. Her rage grew. Then the face of the one who pushed her through the portal came into view. A deeper frown imprinted itself upon her face.

"I will make you tremble," she screamed, pushing her arms down to her sides hard, her palms parallel to the water. She shot off of the ocean's surface, pulling a jet off water up behind her.

Gravity took hold of the water and pulled it back down. Turning toward land, Sorcea shot toward New Covenant.

# BY REFLEX

Ms. Clark was clad in white leather as she'd been when she saved them from Sorcea. Around her they stood, transformed into their Danger Kids costumes, with the exception of Ray. He was still wearing his school clothes and a smile on his lips as he surveyed the empty white room. The teleportation tickled his stomach and the hairs on his arms were still standing up. At first he felt as if he'd vomit, feeling light headed. Yet, to his surprise the sensations he had felt quickly subsided.

Ms. Clark stared at him for a long moment, placing her hands against her hips. She remembered the first time she teleported and nearly turned a smile. However, the nostalgia quickly wore off as she reminded herself of why they were there in an empty white room.

"Is there something you're waiting for?" Raising her eyebrows, Ms. Clark titled her head to the side, pointing her right ear toward Ray.

"Yeah, uh, I don't think I get the leather spandex," said Ray comically.

"That I'm well aware of."

"So whatever this place is, and whatever we're doing here, let's do it."

"Not until you transform," said Ms. Clark shaking her index finger at Ray.

"Not doing it."

Ms. Clark breathed in deeply through her nose. Snapping her fingers and opening her hand, a large knife appeared in her palm. "I guess

I'll have to force you to transform." In a flash she closed the five feet of distance between herself and Ray, jamming the knife into his gut. The other kids gasped in shock.

Ray groaned, tightening his stomach as he felt the tip of the knife on his flesh. Inside of him stomach he could hear what sounded like metal blocks being piled on top of one another.

Pulling the knife away from his belly, Ms. Clark watched as a sheet of metal began to cover Ray's torso.

"What the heck is wrong with you?" asked Ray with a hard frown, stumbling back a bit. He touched his belly and felt the metal covering. "Whoa!" Again Ms. Clark attacked him, swinging the knife at his face.

*Clank!*

The tip of the knife bounced off of Ray's nose. The metal helmet was shiny. Even Ray's eyes were covered and the others watched as the rest of him became covered in a fabulous armor. As his entire body became encased in a metal armor, a long shaft appeared in front of him, and at the end of it was a large hammerhead. He wrapped his hand around it and a deep humming reverberated as his metal hand came into contact with it.

"Now that's cool," said Anthony nodding his head up and down excited.

"See now, that wasn't so hard," said Ms. Clark flickering her wrist. The knife went flying into the air and disappeared.

"Now will you tell me what we're doing here?" asked Ray, his voice slightly muffled behind his helmet.

"You are here to learn." Ms. Clark began walking around in a circle looking at each of the kids. Swirling her hand around, she eyed each of them as she passed. Her eyes were sharp and calculating as she watched them. As she neared Kareem she whispered a word and a flame burst out and around her hand. Turning from him, she shot the flame at Mirely.

"Uh," Mirely gasped and pulled her hands up, waving them in a circle and then pushed them forward hard. A powerful gust of wind caught the flame and swirled around it. Swinging her hands up, she pushed the swirling wind toward the ceiling, carrying the flame until it dissipated.

"Very good," said Ms. Clark. She continued to walk in a circle.

"Show off," said Kareem to a smiling Mirely.

Turning toward the sound of Kareem's voice Ms. Clark pushed her hands forward and balls of ice flew from them. One ball and then two thudded against Kareem's chest. He stumbled back stunned, falling to one knee. Lifting his head, he saw another three balls of ice flying toward him. Rolling to one side he avoided one. As the next two made their way toward him, he tried to move again, but found himself stuck, unable to control himself. Another ball of ice smacked him in the nose, the other in the chest.

"Not very good," said Ms. Clark as she stood over Kareem. Waving her forefinger as if to beckon him, he floated onto his feet under her control.

Kareem was in pain, holding his chest as he looked down at Ms. Clark.

"This exercise isn't about physical evasion. Just as I have, your enemies can prevent you from being able to move. You must be able to harness and control your energy Kareem." Ms. Clark's eyes left him and he felt ashamed. "Are you ready?"

Aaron was breathing hard, starting intently, and preparing himself for whatever was to come. His heart was pounding in his chest so hard that he could hear it. He wiggled his fingers and then shook his wrists.

"Who is he to call someone a coward?" said Ms. Clark softly to herself as she slowly stepped toward him. As she walked toward him, she pointed her fingers toward him with her palms facing up. The floor began to crunch and break apart. Two large pieces of the floor rose, into the air. Bobbing for a moment in front of her, she kissed her lips at Aaron.

Aaron groaned as the blocks of marble shot toward him. He crouched slowly and his stomach began to tighten. His fists were tight as he tried to summon his powers. His palms flashed bright for a split second, but nothing shot from them. "Ah!" He screamed as he kicked the first block away from him. Turning to the side, he let the other miss him and watched it slam into the wall.

"No moving," said Ms. Clark as she snapped her fingers together at Aaron.

He felt something take hold of him and he couldn't move. He only had power of over his arms and hand, which were being held up at the height of his shoulder.

*Crunch, crunch,* he heard the floor and watched in fear as Ms. Clark launched another block of marble at him.

"Jesus Christ what's wrong with you," said Aaron, his eyes welling as the block neared him. He closed his eyes, not knowing what to do to protect himself.

*Voom!*

Aaron felt a warm wave of energy pass his face and then he heard the marble block shattered. The block fell to the floor in a hundred pieces. The staccato of marble against marble gave Aaron the courage to open his eyes.

"Don't thank me," said Ray with a blasé look on his face.

"No one asked you to interfere," said Ms. Clark giving Ray an angry scowl. Ray smirked at her. Rolling her eyes she moved her hands about and twelve pieces of the floor cracked and rose.

A short smile creased the corner of Ray's mouth as he watched the floating blocks of marble. Ms. Clark screamed pushing both hands forward and the blocks of marble began to swirl around the room. The blocks raced around Ray's head, circling him like vicious predators.

The smile on his face grew longer. One block flew toward him and he dealt with it, shooting a magnetic shockwave from his hammer. Another came and he eradicated it just the same. "How about we up the ante?"

"Much obliged." Ms. Clark clapped her hands together and the ten remaining blocks of marble went rocketing toward Ray.

Grunting, he slammed the staff of his hammer into the floor as the granite blocks raced toward him from the air. A silver forced field rose up from under his feet, wrapping itself around Ray. The blocks of marble collided with the magnetic force field around him and shattered into pieces.

"Good." That's all Ms. Clark would give him for a compliment. "Perhaps a bit arrogant."

"Just confident," he replied.

"I bet." Turning to Anthony, Ms.Clark nodded her head and he nodded in response. His mask folded around his mouth and she knew he was smiling. "Always excited."

"What do I have to do?" asked Anthony, bouncing up and down on the balls of his feet.

Ms. Clark snapped her palms open and five blades appeared, resting in her open hands. "Don't let anyone get hurt." The sentence was slow and imperative, like an order. There was severe warning and dread in Ms. Clark's voice. "Catch!" She yelled, pulling her hands in and whipped her arms out. A blade flew toward the faces of the other five Danger Kids.

Anthony paused for a split second to say "Whoa," and then stood in front of Ms. Clark holding the six blades as her arms came to rest by her sides. "Nobody got hurt," beamed Anthony with a big smile.

Ms Clark's right thumb went up and the blades in Anthony's hands disappeared. "That leaves just one." Turning toward Alex, Ms. Clark wiggled her fingers by her sides like a Wild West gunslinger.

Alex rubbed his hands together and blew into them as if he were cold. He rubbed them again, trying to focus. He didn't know what Ms. Clark was going to do. He knew she wasn't trying to hurt them, so he wasn't afraid. His heart was pounding, but not because of fear. He was afraid to fail. He'd already failed his friends in the moment of truth against Sorcea. Something took over him and he didn't want it to come back now. He wanted it to remain at bay, so that he'd be able to perform as he had when Mirely attacked Ray.

Pressing his mind into his belly, he tried to remember the feeling he'd had in the classroom. It was a nauseating feeling of dread. Though he hadn't known Ray very long, Alex always seemed to have an affinity for people and their safety. He treated everyone the same until their actions forced him to change his mind. More powerful was his hope that his friends would never hurt anyone. Further, he didn't wish any ill will on those who weren't his friends.

"Are you prepared?" Alex heard a soft voice in his head and thought it was Ms. Clark's, but he wasn't entirely sure. When it whispered to him again he knew it was. Blinking his eyes hard, he saw Ms. Clark's arms swinging and bending in circles as if she were performing Tai Chi. '*Can you trust her? Can you trust yourself?*' The voice clouded his mind and his mind moved from his stomach back into is head. His focus was gone and he could no longer connect with the feeling he'd had earlier. He would only trust his eyes and all he could see was Ms. Clark's hands moving in weird ways as her arms swung. He could hear energy swirling about the room, but he couldn't feel it. He was supposed to be able to feel it. He had felt all of the other Danger Kids' energy when they'd used it.

"I will not fail." Alex tried to convince himself that he'd be able to summon his powers when the attack came. The inevitability of Ms. Clark's assault had begun the moment the *Margortis teleportis* spell had brought them to the quiet white room. He'd have to act. Aaron still thought him weak. He had begun to believe Aaron until he stopped Mirely from hurting Ray. '*You will fail.*' The voice entered into his mind again. Pain shot across his head and he closed one eye as he cringed in discomfort.

"Ah!" Ms. Clark's voice was loud. Her arms circled once more and then her hands shot forward. The fingers on her right hand faced the ceiling, while her left faced the floor.

*Swoosh!*

The force of energy exploded out, making a thunderous sound. It erupted in every direction, pushing the kids back as the jet of invisible energy made its way to Alex.

'*Coward,*' the voice in his head said. '*You are faltering. You will fail. You are weak.*' Alex responded by saying *no* to himself, but he believed the voice. He knew he'd failed, he knew he was weak, and he was afraid again. Failure filled his heart. His eyes began to tear and he cried.

*Thump!*

Alex's back slammed hard against the wall. Mirely and Kareem rushed over to him. Alex began lifting himself up from the floor and Kareem grabbed him under the armpit, helping to lift him. Mirely touched his other arm and asked him if he were okay. He lifted a hand to suggest he was fine, but there was a slight limp in his step as he began to move and tears wet on his cheeks.

Anthony blitzed over and Aaron began to walk over. Ray looked at Ms. Clark's sullen face. She seemed disappointed and he wondered why. "Expecting more of him?" Ray's tone was full of accusation and intrigue.

"No more than anyone else," she replied blankly. "Everyone." Ms. Clark beckoned them with open arms, and they slowly gathered around. "Max." The walls shifted to one side of the room and slipped into an opening in the floor. The floor repaired itself and each of the marble blocks tucked itself neatly into its resting place.

"Hey Max," said Mirely happily.

"Good afternoon Danger Kids," said Max in his warm computerized tone.

"Wow a talking a computer," said Ray sarcastically, unimpressed.

"Same thing I thought," said Aaron, trying to be cordial. He knew he and Ray kept getting off on the wrong foot. It seemed that fate had forced them together. He thought that he might as well make the most of it before they were at one another's throats.

"The room we just left was where you'll train every day after school." Ms. Clark marched to Max's control panel and punched a few buttons.

"Our detention," said Kareem annoyed. "This has to be like a little piece of death."

Ms. Clark turned and cut her eye at Kareem. "I assure you that you wont die here."

"I imagined myself old and grey, in my bed, with a big bucket of ice cream," said Kareem looking up imagining the scene.

"Best way to go," said Alex with a smile giving Kareem a high five as he rubbed at his reddening eyes.

"Elwood's probably going to die of fear," said Aaron scoffing loudly.

"Don't start," shot Mirely, giving Aaron the evil eye. She was still angry with him.

"You didn't exactly score any points in the training room," said Kareem, defending Alex as he always did.

"That's exactly what we're here to discuss," said Ms. Clark loudly, quieting everyone. "Whatever problems you people have need to be solved really soon. Quickly even. None of this will help you. There needs to be unity among you." Pressing a button on Max's control panel, Ms. Clark motioned her hand toward the screen.

The crests were lined up on the screen, their symbols glowing. Every ten seconds one would be isolated on the screen, with a name written across it. The kids recognized their names as each crest appeared on the screen.

"These names along with the costumes you wear were given to the first team of Danger Kids. They weren't used to protect their identities because it was an honor to be a Danger Kid. Everyone in Atlantis knew who the Danger Kids were. Of course times have changed and the world is different." Ms. Clark sounded elegant but weary. Her voice was heavy as if a great sadness had overtaken her. "The Danger Kids were trained for many years to develop their power. There was no imminent threat when Mysticgo endowed them with their abilities. Sadly you do not have that luxury."

Ms. Clark breathed in deeply and then titled her head back, closing her eyes and breathing in again. "Mirely, you are called Skyrain, and you can summon weather of all kinds. You could call upon a light drizzle, a hard rain, a torrential downpour, snowstorm, blizzard; or even a hurricane or tornado. Your powers are tied directly to your emotion and therefore it is easy for you to summon them. Whenever you are angry or struck with grief or even fear, things like what happened in the classroom will happen. But much of what happened was not under your control. The more you feed into your anger, the less control you'll have. Whatever emotions you are feeling with take over your consciousness and drive you to an end that could be catastrophic to everyone around you."

Kareem cut in. "That doesn't sound like she doesn't have control?"

"You are right Kareem. But she could easily lose it," answered Ms. Clark sharply. Her tone was a warning to him of the devastation her power could cause. Yet, she was staring at Mirely when she said it. Mirely's eyes narrowed as she began to think about what Ms. Clark was saying.

"How do we get control?" asked Alex curious.

"By controlling your emotions," said Ray as if everyone should have figured it out by now.

"That helps a lot," said Aaron with a scowl.

"You need all the help you can get." Ray was laughing as he said it, knowing it would infuriate Aaron. Aaron's fists were balled as he turned toward Ray.

"What's your issue?" begged Aaron ready to pounce.

"I don't have an issue," replied Ray with a smile.

"You must, you've always got something to say about me."

"No issue."

Aaron turned from Ray and looked at Ms. Clark who was staring at him shaking her head. Disappointment was all over her face and Aaron turned his eyes from her when he recognized it.

For a few moments, Ms. Clark stared at the side of Aaron's head and then focused her attention on Ray. "Humph," she uttered. "While he is supremely confident, borderline arrogant, and terribly annoying. Ray who is called Metalix, unlike Mirely is completely in control of his emotions. He also possesses the advantage of having powers that are also physically based. The metal in and around his body acts as a conductor for his magnetic abilities."

Ray stuck out his chest, full of pride as Ms. Clark complimented his ability to control his powers.

"Anthony's not exactly stable, but he doesn't have any problems," said Kareem pointing at Anthony as if he'd done something wrong.

Alex looked at Kareem as he jarred and questioned Ms. Clark. His eyes were wide and full of wonder. He wanted to know. Anthony wasn't the smartest among them. He always seemed absent minded. However, like Ray and Mirely, he was able to summon his powers at will.

"It's because he doesn't think," said Ms. Clark.

"So thinking is bad?" asked Alex.

"In a way. Up until now all of you have been using your powers by reflex. Acting only when your lives are in danger; or in the case of Alex in the classroom, when another's life was in danger. As you thought earlier, when there was no imminent danger, knowing I wouldn't kill you, you hesitated Alex."

Alex was floored. "Could you read my mind?" he begged.

"One of my skills like yours is telepathy."

"So you were in my head telling me things?"

"No," said Ms. Clark with a confused stare. She looked down at the floor, moving her head from one side to another, her mouth moving, but no sound coming form them.

"But that doesn't explain me," said Kareem.

"You're Fryo," said Ms. Clark sternly to Kareem. "While fire may seem vicious, angry, and vengeful, it comes from a place of quiet, calm, and serenity. It takes patience to kindle a fire in the woods. Wood burns slowly until the fire spreads. Thunder and Lightning work in concert, as a storm brews Aaron. It isn't immediate. Though the Thunderbolt moves with tremendous speed and destructive force. The right elements need to be in place for it to work. Anthony, who is called Chrono does not have these problems. His powers are all physically based. His thoughtlessness is his strength. He simply acts."

"Got it now?" asked Ray of Aaron sarcastically. Aaron gave him a hard look and gritted his teeth, pulling in his lips. "Now you're learning." Ray continued to egg him on.

"But my name's Dark Shadow," said Alex. He looked confused as he questioned the name on the screen that covered his crest. "Everyone's name kind of makes sense for their powers. I don't see where my name makes any sense."

"You've got shadow powers," said Kareem swaying his hands about. His voice grew deep as if he were a host for an old horror film.

"Seriously," said Alex, knocking at Kareem's hands.

"You possess abilities of the mind. They are telekinesis, telepathy, and gravity manipulation. Thus above all the others, you have to be both in control your emotions and in control of you mind. It sounds weird, but you'll soon understand the feeling. It'll become second nature." Ms. Clark smiled to try and put Alex's mind at ease.

"That sounds like a lot," said Kareem to Alex.

Aaron was shaking his head *no* and Ray stepped closer to him. Ray wrapped his arm around Aaron's shoulder and caressed the ball of his shoulder. "You'll get it too thunder puff." A big smile was on Ray's face when he said it.

"Prick!" Aaron swung with all his might and punched Ray in the ribs. The metal covering Ray's body sung a soft song. "Uh!" Aaron screamed, feeling intense pain in his knuckles. He rubbed and shook his hand, hoping it'd relieve the pain.

"Better luck next time," said Ray, walking away laughing hard.

"You don't have to taunt him," said Mirely as Ray neared her.

He was still smiling from ear to ear. "He deserved it for what he said." Mirely melted and rolled her eyes, as she begged her cheeks not to turn read.

"Are we ready for another go at it?" asked Ms. Clark of the entire group.

"Might as well learn now. I might live to die in my bed," said Kareem looking indifferent.

"Max," said Ms. Clark and the wall rose up from the floor and began to fold out. The control room disappeared from sight and the white walls were their only other company. "Who's first?"

# PANDEMONIUM

Mirely zipped behind Alex and lifted him by the back of his collar. Spinning hard, she whipped her arms and sent him flying into the air. With a wave of her hand, a short cyclone of air settled in under Alex and wrapped itself around him. Pointing her forefinger into the air, the cyclone shot up and she waved her finger in a circle and the cyclone began to spin faster.

A smirked lined Mirely's face as she listened to Alex yell at the top of his lungs. His arms and legs were flailing about as he tried to right himself, but it didn't help. Mirely twirled her finger again and the cyclone spun even faster.

The other kids ran and slipped out the way as the cyclone jagged around the room.

"You have to focus," said Ms. Clark, yelling to Alex. She hoped he could hear her. Mirely had bested the entire team, but Alex was fairing the worst. He hadn't managed to use his powers the entire five minutes that they'd dueled. Even Kareem managed to get three shots in on her.

"Down you go," said Mirely in a spirited voice as she closed her hand. The cyclone dissipated and Alex hit the floor in a heap.

"Ugh." Alex landed on his shoulder and rolled onto his back. He tried to stand slowly, but wobbled hard as he stood and pitched sideways hitting the floor again. Grabbing at his stomach, he filled his mouth with air, forcing the sickness back into his stomach.

"Take it easy," said Kareem kneeling over him and pressing a hand to his chest.

The rest of the group gathered around Alex and watched him suck in air. He closed his eyes when he saw everyone with sullen and surprised expressions looking at him. His mind was blank and he thought about his epic failure. He inhaled deeply and exhaled for a long moment.

"Are you okay?" asked Mirely.

Kareem burst into laughter, clapping his hands as his concern for Alex began to wane. He knew he'd be ok as he watched his friend sit up slowly, his eyes still closed tightly together.

"Seriously?" Alex opened his eyes and he could see Kareem's hysteria. It was all too close to him and he could feel his warm breath on his face as he continued to laugh.

Aaron and Anthony tried to present a look of indifference but failed at it. Their lips were pulled back against their teeth, hoping to keep their laughter in. Only Mirely and Ms. Clark seemed concerned and Ray appeared to be somewhat disappointed.

"It's ok," said Alex as he stared at Aaron and Anthony for a while. They finally burst into loud obnoxious laughter after looking at one another.

"Let me help you," begged Kareem, standing and giving his hand for Alex to grab a hold of.

"You're so kind." Alex took Kareem's hand and stood up with his friend's help.

"How does it feel being handled by a girl?" asked Aaron with a big smile. He took pleasure in watching Alex get beaten.

"I don't remember you winning anything."

"I didn't finish with a big fat zero."

"What does that even mean?" Alex tried to act as if he didn't know.

"You didn't even lay a finger on her," said Kareem nearly screaming, incredulous that Alex would ask that question. "Are you out of your mind? Are you sick?" Kareem touched his palm to Alex's head and then reached down and felt for a pulse.

Alex slapped Kareem's hands away. "Really?

"What went wrong?" asked Ms. Clark, putting an end to the tumult and jokes. She wasn't laughing or smiling, and looked to be concerned.

Her looked seemed to knock the air out of Alex as she stepped closer to him.

"I'm not quite sure," he replied.

"Could you hear me?" asked Ms. Clark, looking into Alex's eyes.

"I could hear just fine."

"I meant could you hear my voice?"

"It's pretty hard to focus when you're getting thrown around Ms. Clark," said Alex letting out a little laugh, hoping she would join in as the others had.

Cold. Her face was a mask of stone cold seriousness that forced Alex to swallow hard.

"While this may seem like fun and games, it is not." Her eyes remained locked with Alex's for what seemed like a long moment to him and then she turned to the others as she began again. "Sorcea will kill everyone of you to get your crests for Dorigon. This isn't child's play anymore."

"But we are children," said Kareem, never missing a moment to infect the air with his sarcasm.

"You are children whose lives are in danger." Ms. Clark shook her head in frustration. Setting her hands on her hips, she breathed out deeply. Twice she did it to calm herself before she began again. "Your predecessors had years of training before they were ready to face Dorigon. Lose they did many times before coming close to defeating him and his servants. And when they got closer, he grew more and more powerful. What do you think would have happened to you if I hadn't show up to save you?"

The room grew silent and the question lingered there unanswered. They all knew the answer, but as they looked at one another, it became clear that none of them wanted to answer it. Mirely's lips were shaking, anger and sadness gripping her at once. Ms. Clark stared at her and smiled.

"Even you would have been killed."

Mirely closed her eyes softly and turned her head to the side. She didn't want to look at Ms. Clark and the white floor was far more appealing at this moment. She knew it was the truth. As much as she was able to use her power, beating her friends and beating Sorcea were two entirely different matters. Sorcea was going to subdue her eventually. Alex was no help and Ray wasn't even a Danger Kid yet. "I know." Mirely whispered, but it was loud enough for everyone to hear. She'd grown confident in her powers and each time she faced her friends in a duel she'd won.

"No one's denying that," said Aaron trying to come to Mirely's rescue. She just rolled her eyes at him.

"Tell us what to do." Alex begged. The laughter had helped to quiet his disappointment, but he felt it rising again. In the classroom, everyone looked to him for help. Now, he felt helpless. "Take yourself less seriously," said Anthony with a big smile, bouncing up and down. He zipped around the room twice in less than five seconds. "Have a little bit of fun."

*Thwack!*

Aaron slapped him on the back of the head and offered him a frown, shushing him, his forefinger pressed against his lips.

"No, he's smarter than his test scores might suggest." They all laughed. That was a rare show of humor from Ms. Clark.

"See." Anthony jutted his eyebrows up and down, swinging at Aaron's head and missing by a mile.

"Easy dork face," said Aaron, pointing his finger at Anthony in a commanding way.

"Mr. Elmwood, take position there," said Ms. Clark pointing behind Alex. "Everyone else, around the edge." Ms. Clark moved toward the center of the room and stood across from Alex.

"Good luck bud." Kareem gave Alex a military salute, skipping back toward the wall with a giant smile on his face.

"Thanks."

Alex cracked his knuckles as he watched Ms. Clark settle into place and wiggle her fingers. Alex balled his fists tight in anticipation of what she'd do. '*Quiet your mind*', said a voice in his head. Fear took him for a second, but he quickly realized it was Ms. Clark's voice. He blinked hard and fast, trying to calm himself. He felt like his privacy was being invaded. '*Push me out of your mind,*' Ms. Clark's voice said to him.

Alex grunted as she began to delve into his mind. His forehead was lined with hard wrinkles. '*Waffles for breakfast.*' His eyes popped out of his head as she named the food he'd eaten in the morning. *'Blue Superman underwear.'* His eyes flew open wider and he nearly closed his legs and covered himself.

"Get a grip," he told himself aloud.

*'Focus.'* Ms. Clark's voice barked loud in his head. She could see that his mind was crowded. Alex was flustered and she forced herself deeper into his mind. She began to speak aloud. "The girl that you like-,"

"No!" He screamed, his mild baritone shrieking like nails against a chalkboard. "Please don't." He pleaded and tears welled in his eyes.

"You want to take her to the Winter Holiday Dance," said Ms. Clark aloud with pleasure. She listened names the others whispered. She laughed inside as the others got it wrong. *'Focus or I'll tell everyone.'*

Alex closed his eyes hard, trying to slow his mind, but it raced. He tried to hide the name of the girl, but it kept rushing back to the front of his mind. It was as if Ms. Clark was pulling it out of him and he began trying to pull back. *'Please don't,'* he thought, trying to push the request toward Ms. Clark's mind, but he felt himself being forced away. Alex fell to one knee.

"You think she'll say no don't you." She felt his fear grow and felt some pressure against her mind. Ms. Clark smiled and forced herself deeper. *'I already have that one. Who's this other?'* She knew the name. She'd already seen the girl's face. She wanted to help him fight her. "Both of them can't go with you. And if the first one says no, you can't ask the other. Choices Mr. Elmwood, choices."

"Stop!" he yelled, dropping onto his other knee.

"Her name is…" Ms. Clark began and then a loud ringing began and red lights began to swirl around the room.

Max's voice entered into the room and Ms. Clark turned around hard. The screens lit up all around the room and there were a dozen news stations broadcasting the same disturbance.

"Oh my gosh," said Mirely as she looked at the screen in disbelief."

"Ugh." Alex gasped and dropped to his knees. He fell forward on his hands breathing hard. He felt spent, as if he'd exerted himself physically. Never had he been so tired, nearly heaving as he blinked hard and fast. He looked up at the screen, his eyes going wide with surprise. His disdain for Ms. Clark was suffocated as he saw the news.

"That one," said Ms. Clark pointing to one of the screens.

"I've never seen anything like this," said the black haired news anchor with green eyes. "It's complete pandemonium here at City Hall as police race to try and save the mayor who's hanging from the top of the building."

"Whoa," said Aaron shocked as he saw Sorcea blast two police officers, sending them flying into a cruiser.

"We've got to do something," said Anthony looking around.

"Finally. I've yet to meet this Sorcea," said Ray with a hungry smile on his face.

"Wait, isn't that Crystal?" asked Kareem pointing at the screen seeing Crystal in the throng of the disturbance with a camera in her hand.

Mirely's mouthed popped open in surprise. "What is she doing down there?" She moved closer to the screens and turned hard on Ms. Clark alarmed. "We've got to do something, that's my cousin."

# YOU NEED TO MOVE

C rystal held down the shutter button on her camera, taking pictures in rapid succession. She'd take three shots and shift her view, repeating the process over and over again. Her face was a mass of focus, as she watched the scene unfold before her.

The police car in front of her had a large dent in the hood. The windshield was shattered but unbroken. The doors to the car were open, officers taking cover behind them. One of the officers was barking something she couldn't make out, while the other screamed back, "I didn't sign up for this."

"Whoa!" A police officer went flying past her, slamming through the windshield of a car. Crystal turned and took half a dozen pictures of the officer peeling himself from the window. The side of his head was cut by a piece of glass. She watched him roll from the squad car and slip behind the trunk.

Sirens wailed in the distance, closing in on the historic building in the heart of downtown New Covenant. Three cars rolled toward the front staircase, screeching to a halt. Two officers jumped out of each card, taking cover behind the doors.

"Hey kid, get out of here!" An officer screamed at Crystal waving his hand for her to move. She curled her lips in disgust and scoffed. "Kid what are you doing?" He screamed at her again and she realized she was standing in the middle of the street, surrounded by a dozen or more police cars.

"I'm an investigative reporter, and I've a right to be here just like any of the other reporters on scene," said Crystal in a matter of fact away, pointing to the news vans lined up behind the fray. She even saw her idol Jessica Duarte standing to the right of her. "So why don't you lay off and do your job."

The officer pulled his head back and looked in both directions. He blinked fast and then snapped back to his senses. Jumping up from behind the car door he grabbed Crystal by the arm and began dragging her away from City Hall. She fought against his grip but he was way too strong.

"You must be out of your mind kid. Call your parents and go home," he barked at her as he swung her onto the sidewalk, opposite the building.

Crystal swung her arm up and down with each word, her fist balled up tight. "I will not be man handled by you, I have my rights...wait, what's your badge number. 2456. I'll be filing a detailed complaint about your behavior-,"

*Boom!*

A crashing sound followed by an explosion interrupted her tirade as she was pulled down and shielded by the officer. Crystal cringed as she scraped her knee on the grey concrete and pressed her head against the officer's ribs. Looking behind him, she saw one of the police cars on fire.

The officer shielding her stood and turned around, aiming his gun toward a woman levitating just above the staircase of the building who was holding the mayor by the collar.

"Come any closer and I'll snap his neck," said the woman with jet-black hair blowing in the light breeze.

Crystal recognized her immediately as she grew closer to the ground. It was the same woman from the park, she was sure of it. "Wait this is really happening," she said to herself dumbstruck. People weren't supposed to be able to fly and small women weren't supposed to be able to hold adult men by the neck with one hand. "This is unreal." She spoke to herself in a whisper and lifted her camera slow. She began snapping pictures, zooming in, turning her lens and making adjustments to get the perfect shot. "I should probably go home. Let the crime fighters handle this. No one really likes the mayor any way," she spoke softly to herself holding her camera against her chest. Looking over to her right, she saw her idol Jessica Duarte pointing and waving at her cameraman. Jessica was moving closer to City Hall. "Jessica didn't' get a Pulitzer Prize from running and I want my Pulitzer." Crystal took another shot and began jogging in the direction behind the police cars toward Jessica.

A deep voice swept into the air, magnified by a blowhorn and Crystal could hear him the man addressing Sorcea. "...of the New Covenant Police Department. Please release the mayor into our custody. Or we'll be forced to use deadly-," as he spoke the man suddenly went stiff. His body was covered in a glowing field of purple energy.

Crystal snapped another picture and rounded a car and suddenly she realized how close she was to the action. The frozen police officer was just ten feet from her. For a moment she wondered if she should move back, but then saw her idol, Jessica Duarte brush past her.

"You!" said Sorcea aloud, pointing her forefinger at Jessica Duarte.

Crystal looked at Jessica shocked and then to Sorcea.

"Me," said Jessica stammering over the word.

"Tell your cameraman to point his camera here and make sure that I can be heard," said Sorcea swiftly.

"Marley." Jessica whispered out of fear, her throat rumbling as she tried to get his attention. Marley was taking footage of the entire scene, panning back and forth in several directions. Big headphones were on his ears and Jessica realized she wasn't using her microphone. "Marley," she said loudly.

"Yeah," said Marley whispering.

"Look at me Marley," she said with a smile.

"Yeah." Marley pointed the camera at Jesscia and stuck up his left thumb. "Ready?"

"Marley."

"Yeah?"

"Point the camera at the flying lady please."

"Sure thing boss," he said pointing the camera toward Sorcea.

"Make sure that you can hear her."

"Sure thing."

"A man of few words," said Crystal, staring at the side of Jessica Duarte's head.

Jessica looked at Crystal out of the corner of her eye and frowned. She was confused why a kid was standing next to her. Jessica's face folded into an expression that said *whatever*, and she pointed her microphone toward Sorcea.

"Good," said Sorcea, once the camera and microphone were focused on her. Descending, she pulled the mayor directly in front her. "Danger Kids. You have two minutes before I tear the mayor and this pretty little town apart. Dorigon wants you and there is nothing you can do but comply."

Crystal hadn't stopped snapping photographs since Sorcea began descending. She was in a zone, focused on her task. Her mind raced, as she thought about how she'd tell the story. Only the perfect angle mattered. She believed that a picture was worth a thousand words. She didn't recognize Sorcea staring at her with a frown, and she thought then that a facial expression was worth more than a picture. In real time a face had all the elements of a picture, only she could feel the energy of it somehow.

Crystal felt a powerful force slam into her back and found her throat trapped in Sorcea's hand.

"I'll kill this one first."

The black tunnel between time and space reminded Mirely of a subway station. It was dark as night, and every few moments a light would flash. Teleporting had been fun before. The feeling of being pushed and pulled at once was exhilarating for her. The trip was faster than any mode of transpiration known to man. Yet, this particular trip seemed to drag on longer than it needed to. A portion of New Covenant was just above Aqua Max, albeit under water. *Faster* she thought to herself.

'*We'll get there in time.*' Mirely heard Alex's voice enter into her mind. His words were comforting, but she didn't trust Sorcea. Mirely didn't know her well enough to guess if she'd keep her word. From what she could tell, Sorcea was the kind of person who would ask questions, long after the fight was done.

Sunlight crept into her vision as she heard everyone take in a deep breath. Whether they shot out of the teleportation tunnel, or were pushed through, the trip always ended with a jolt. She exhaled short and hard and then turned her shoulders toward the golden dome of City Hall shining in the distance. She shot toward it like a ball out of a cannon. Anthony's feet hit the ground and he took off in the same direction, quickly gaining ground and then passing Mirely.

"They must be trying to get killed," said Kareem shaking his head *no*.

"Her cousin's there," said Ray in a matter of fact tone.

"Let's just get there and help," said Alex quickly diffusing the tension in the group.

"Should we run?" asked Aaron looking at the distance between them and City Hall. It was at least a half-mile.

"I've got a better idea," said Ray, opening his arms.

The boys felt a vibration under them and then saw a mass of energy wrapping itself around them. As the mass of energy grew encircling them, it buzzed louder until they were all encased in a force field of magnetic energy.

"Ready," said Ray, muffled behind his helmet.

"Ready," they said in unison.

Ray pulled them up into the air and began flying toward City Hall.

"If you ever learn how to use your powers, you should be able to fly too," said Aaron sarcastically to Alex with a smirk.

Alex cringed and wanted to respond, but he feared getting into a back and forth that he couldn't win. Other than communicate telepathically, he wasn't sure what he'd be able to do against Sorcea. For some reason, he felt like he was the only one among them who didn't want to take action and fight. He'd rather be home reading a book. His love for his friends was the only thing keeping him there.

"Stay behind me and watch my back," said Kareem winking an eye at him. Alex smiled happily. "Just don't try to hold my hand."

"Promise."

"Sorcea!" Mirely roared, her soft voice screeching as she yelled. "Let her go!" Her rage rose up in her chest and a bolt of lightning crackled across the blue sky.

A wicked smile crept across Sorcea's face as she saw Mirely flying toward her. "Where are your friends?" She yelled the question, but there was no rage in her voice. A mild ferocity held sway over Sorcea's voice. Her eyes were sharp and focused as she watched the pixie-like Danger Kid make her way toward her.

"Don't you worry about them, just let her go."

"A trade then. These worms for you and your friends to come with me to answer to Lord Dorigon."

"How about you let her go and I don't break you in half," said Mirely as she landed, standing face to face with Sorcea.

"My - my - my, even more confident than before." Sorcea was somewhat shocked, but she was mostly amused, releasing a huff of air as she smiled. "Seems your friend still hasn't quite found any balance or sense of direction."

Anthony was peeling himself off the ground, kicking a newspaper stand to the side.

Mirely looked for a short moment, and quickly turned her attention back to Sorcea. She didn't care about Anthony's balance, only her cousin's safety. The mayor was playing second fiddle. She'd taken no oaths of office or duty.

Jessica Duarte was standing in close proximity to Sorcea and Mirely, her microphone pointing toward them. Marley was taping, capturing what he thought made sense, and following every order Jessica Duarte gave him with head and hand signals.

The cops behind Mirely were still taking cover behind their car doors, while one of them stood with a blowhorn. He seemed to be waiting for something to happen and hadn't spoken in quite sometime.

Mirely looked over her shoulder and saw all the people gathered on the opposite sidewalk. For their safety she was afraid and wished they'd go home. She thought it would be better for them to be tucked away on a sofa than to stand witness to Sorcea's cruelty. She took account of the police officers. She thought of them as allies rather than defenseless witnesses. How much help they'd be she wasn't sure. She wasn't even sure if she and her friends could take Sorcea down.

"I can feel your apprehension," said Sorcea with a snarl.

Turning to Jessica Duarte, Mirely hissed to get her attention. Her face was focused on Sorcea as she spoke. "You might want to get away from here."

"I'm a reporter. It is my duty to uh-!" Jessica gasped as Mirely grabbed her arm by the wrist.

"You need to move." The urgency in her voice was harsh and though Jessica couldn't see her eyes, they were stern and piercing enough that Jessica could sense their intensity. Slowly Jessica began moving back, snapping her finger and twirling her arm for Marley to move and take a different vantage point.

The wind howled to Mirely's left and she looked, but didn't see anything. Her hair flew across her face and over her right shoulder. Her wings flapped involuntarily as a strong gust of wind whipped past her. She heard Sorcea gasp and grunt at once.

"I got the mayor!" said Anthony as he began to slow down and come into focus. "Oh!" He pitched forward and hit the ground in a heap.

*Crunch!*

"Crud." Anthony grunted as the mayor landed on top of him, face to face. "This isn't how I imagined we'd meet Mayor Cross"

Mayor William Cross looked at Anthony quizzically, hearing a voice coming from behind the boy's mask. "Thank you." The mayor stood up slowly and began fixing his suit. As he pulled down at his suit jacket, he watched Anthony stand up slowly and look around. "And you are?"

"Chrono sir, of the Danger Kids," said Anthony happily, sticking out his hand for a handshake.

"Chrono?"

"You got it," he said looking up seeing Ray flying overhead with the others. "And those are my pals."

"The Danger Kids?"

"Yup!"

"Who exactly are the Danger Kids?" asked Mayor Cross with a discerning twist of his neck.

"We're the good guys sir."

"But you're just kids," said Mayor Cross with a look of concern.

"Heroes come in all sizes," said Anthony as a group of officers began to converge on the mayor. "You guys take it from here." Anthony waved at the officers and then zipped back toward Mirely.

"All six of you are here," said Sorcea. She was still holding a teary eyed Crystal, her forearm tucked neatly under Crystal's neck as she watched Ray and the others touched down from the air. Anthony zipped past them and came to a sudden stop give feet away. He balanced himself on his toes, trying to make sure that he didn't fall again. Sorcea smiled with pleasure at his feat and watched him strut over to the rest of the group.

"Would you mind letting her go?" asked Anthony of Sorcea.

She gave him the evil eye and he cringed.

"I didn't imagine you would," said Anthony turning to the other Danger Kids. "I think we should probably try to do something to sort this kidnapping thing out."

"Will you shut up?" said Kareem.

"You've got us here, now let the girl go," said Alex stepping to the front of the pack.

"Such bravery." Sorcea began to laugh at Alex, tilting her head back slightly. "I had thought that such courage was confined to the girl and the lunatics of your little gang. That would obviously excludes you...what was it?"

Alex grimaced at her statement, his lips curling into resentful scowl. "Dark Shadow." He said his name with pride and force.

"So you've all taken the names of the ancients that came before you? How quaint." Sorcea's smirk was packed with revulsion and annoyance.

"Why are we still talking?" asked Ray looking around at everyone. He hadn't stopped moving since they landed. He was itching for a fight the moment he laid eyes on Sorcea.

"Because she has her." Mirely answered swiftly, cutting her eye at him. "She's innocent...so let her go."

"A trade, is that what you're offering?" asked Sorcea of Mirely.

"No what I think she's asking for is mercy." Ray smiled as she spoke and slowly began to chuckle. "You let the girl go and we wont beat the crap out of you."

"What would stop me from snapping her neck now," said Sorcea tightening her grip on Crystal.

Crystal began to choke and her eyes began to water. She coughed and clawed at Sorcea's arm, but her grip didn't loosen.

"Please, no, stop!" Mirely's voice cracked as her hands shot forward in submission. She believed Sorcea was mad enough to act on her words. If something happened to Crystal she'd blame herself.

"A friend? Family? Which one is it? Someone you in particular obviously care for. You had no concern for the safety of the mayor." Sorcea smiled deviously, loosing the suffocating grip around Crystal's throat.

"She's innocent like she said." Ray's sternly, his voice growing deep.

"Then a trade Mr. Mercy," said Sorcea full of authority. "You for the girl."

"Please let me go," said Crystal. "I didn't do anything wrong."

"Hush now child. The deal is nearly struck."

"Help me please," begged Crystal, looking directly at Alex. "I don't want to die."

Crystal's words crashed into Alex. His heart began to beat rapidly and his mind began to race. The lack of control he'd felt the first day they faced Sorcea took over him. His failure in the training room played like a movie in front of his eyes. The voice in his head began to talk to him again. It reminded him that the only quality he possessed was weakness. The voice told him to submit, to let himself be taken over, so that he could become more.

Alex dropped to his knees holding his hands to his ears. "Get out of my head," said Alex aloud.

Ray looked down at him concerned, keeping watch of Sorcea out of the corner of his eyes.

"Not again, not now, in front of everyone," said Aaron looking around at the throng of people that had gathered around to watch the scene unfold. Police, news, and what seemed like the entire city.

"The weakness returns," said Sorcea giggling.

"Get a grip," said Kareem without turning his attention from Sorcea.

"Focus dude," said Ray.

Alex grabbed Ray by the wrist and pulled him down toward him. Alex was in pain, his right hand still covering his ear.

"Whatever you do, don't make the trade, she'll kill her any way. I could hear her thinking about it." Alex screamed aloud trying to clear his head.

"Well what you do you want us to do?" Ray's eyes were bulging behind his helm when Alex said *do nothing*. He wasn't as brash as he led on, but wasn't sure he could just stand by and do nothing.

"Trust me, I have a plan." Alex fell forward, both hands touching the cold pavement. "Do what I do."

"Are you crazy?" begged Ray, screaming and whispering at once. His voice was a high-pitched airy thing that only Alex could hear. He surely didn't want any girls to hear his voice that way.

"Just do it," said Alex and then his voice crept into the minds of the other. *Everyone* he said to them psychically.

"What are we doing?" asked Aaron shocked and amazed as the Danger Kids kneeled down, lowering their heads to Sorcea. "Are you out of your mind?"

"Bow Aaron!" said Alex in the harshest tone he could muster.

"It's called supplication boy," said Sorcea with a huge smile. "Do as your weakling leader commands."

Aaron frowned at Sorcea and wanted nothing more than to press his fist into her face. He'd never hit a girl before, but she was asking for it.

Slowly Aaron kneeled, still facing Sorcea with his hard stare. Turning his head to his right, he looked harder at Alex. "You better not screw this up Elmwood." He whispered to himself and thought the same sentence. He was sure Sorcea couldn't hear him, but he was sure that Alex could read his mind.

'*Trust me, I promise we'll save her.*'

# DEACTIVATE

Alex's eyes were closed as he concentrated his mind toward the other Danger Kids. He felt Aaron bend forward and place his hands onto the ground. The sensation intrigued him, as his connection with each of his friends became much more intimate. A feeling of alarm washed over him as he thought that he could control their bodies. He thought that no one should be able to lose control of him or herself at the hands of another. Then he wondered what Ms. Clark was able to do, knowing her mental powers were much greater than his own. The thought frightened him.

He thought to try and enter Sorcea's mind and then quickly dispensed with the idea. He figured if she were a telepath they'd know by now. Each one of them would be on a hook in whatever mystical slaughterhouse she'd concoct. Alex also guessed that she knew how to shield herself from psychic attack.

Quickly he pushed his mind toward Crystal and entered into her mind. It was easy, taking very little effort. The Danger Kids had proved difficult because they were ready for him to try. They'd been taught how to put up psychic barriers. His own psychic barrier was stronger than any of his friends, yet the only person that could enter his mind was Ms. Clark. Alex didn't stand a chance, and neither did Crystal.

His mind began to form the words that he'd say and he watched as a startled look took over her face. Crystal could feel something inside her head, but couldn't figure out what it was. It was a sensation similar to a headache without the pain. Her brain was tingling and she wondered if she were dying.

'No-,' thought Alex to Crystal and quickly stopped himself. It occurred to him that she'd know the sound of his voice, since his telepathic voice sounded the same as his physical voice. They'd been friends since first grade. There was no way he could use his own physical voice. It would give his identity away and he'd have a lot of explaining to do.

"What?" Crystal said aloud hearing as voice in her head and nearly began to panic.

*'Keep cool, I'm going to get you out of this,'/* thought Alex to Crystal. *'Don't speak, think back to me, just as if we were talking.'* Alex's telepathic voice was a deep baritone he'd been practicing in the shower when he acted like a king from the middle ages.

*'Who are you...where are you...how are you in my head? Oh my God I'm freaking out. This chick's off her rocker. I can't die now. I haven't won my Pulitzer yet. I swear if I don't get into Harvard my mother will just die-,'* thought Crystal, quickly forgetting that someone was talking to her psychically. Her future flashed before her eyes. Her hopes and dreams, the hopelessness her mother would feel all suddenly became real. What would her mom do without her? She didn't want to think about it.

*'I'm Dark Shadow. I'm going to try and get you out of this, but I need your help.'*

*'Please just do something, anything.'*

"Now you will all deactivate your crests," said Sorcea as she slid her forearm from under Crystal's throat and quickly grabbed her by the back of the neck.

"Ouch lady, what's wrong with you?" begged Crystal in pain.

Sorcea jerked her backward and then pushed her forward, extending her arm. She barked an order at Crystal. "Shut up girl."

"Was your mother a psychopath or something?" asked Crystal seriously.

*'Deactivate guys,'* thought Alex to the Danger Kids.

*'You've gone mad,'* thought Aaron to Alex.

Kareem thought with a chuckle. *'Lost his noodles for sure.'*

'*We'll be defenseless against her,*' thought Ray shaking his head *no*.

"I promise you, it will be alright. You'll be able to go back to your normal lives as kids. My Lord Dorigon will see that you are all rewarded for your fealty," said Sorcea to Ray who she thought was shaking his head *no* at the thought of losing his powers.

"We'll comply," said Dark Shadow craning his neck to meet Sorcea's eyes.

"The weakest are always the most apt to lead with rational thought," said Sorcea with a satisfied smile.

'*Get ready Crystal. When I say go, I want you to give her your best elbow shot.*'

'*Are you mad? She'll kill me? I'm not a hero. I'm a reporter. Aren't you masked freaks supposed to be the ones saving the day? Are you trying to get me killed...*' thought Crystal and she continued to think about all the awful ways she would die.

Alex didn't try to interrupt her. He knew her too well and she'd only enter into another self-serving monologue about why his plan was crazy. Her way was the only way and anyone who tried to have it another way always suffered. Well, mostly their ears.

'*If you don't get away from her, we can't help you. We need you to create a window for us to act. We can't risk it while she still has you or you're dead any way,*' thought Alex hoping Crystal would see things his way.

'*What like a diversion or something?*'

'*Exactly.*'

"Who'd like to go first?" asked Sorcea, moving Crystal in front of Aaron, staring at the back of his head over the girl's shoulder.

Aaron lifted his hands from off of the ground a sat back on his heels. He turned his eyes toward Sorcea and a grimace secured control of his lips. Hate and rage boiled within him. He wanted to introduce her to the bolt of lightning radiating just under the surface of his palm.

"There is always a hot head who spoils everything. Life for this girl will cease to exist." Sorcea's hand began to glow a dark purple and Crystal screamed in pain. The police behind them began to scream in pain, grabbing at their chests on the left side, dropping to their knees. "Who will protect this city if the boys in blue are no longer here? Surely the Danger Kids can't be everywhere all the time. You have a chance to survive, but these people do not."

The radiating bolt of energy crackled around his hand. It raged more within his hand as he balled his fist. Hot streaks of fire zipped from the ends of the lightning energy buzzing around his hand.

"Lightning Fire, now isn't that interesting. You're strong, but obviously out of control," said Sorcea disgusted.

"Aaron!" Anthony grabbed Aaron's left wrist and squeezed.

"Get off," shot Aaron turning to face Anthony.

Anthony recoiled slightly, pulling his head back on his shoulders as if Aaron's breath were bad. He was still afraid of Aaron. He'd stuffed him in enough lockers with Brick to still be scary, even with his new powers. Anthony leaned in fast and whispered into Aaron's ear. "Elwood's got a plan."

"You trust Dorkwood?"

"I've never failed at anything he's helped me with," said Anthony cheerfully.

Alex listened to the exchange mentally. He'd known about Anthony's admiration for a long time. He never knew it ran so deep.

*'I promise you'll get to hit her first Aaron.'*

Aaron was tough as nails, and he'd never backed down from a fight in his short young life. He'd never been intimidated by bigger boys. He hated bullies, and stuffing people in lockers was as far as his terror went. He stood up for people who couldn't protect themselves, even against his own friends. Sorcea was a bully. Backing down from her went against everything he believed in and everything he stood for. Crystal wasn't his friend, but he knew her well enough and she couldn't protect herself. All he wanted to do was shoot his bolt of lightning at Sorcea. Staring in her eyes made what Alex was asking him to do even more difficult. The enjoyment she'd get from watching him submit was already in her moist eyes. The smile she'd show him he already hated.

Aaron felt Anthony tug at him again and when he turned to look at the smaller boy he could hear the fear in him when he said "Come on."

Biting the inside of his bottom lip, he turned back to Sorcea with rage in his eyes. She watched him intently and then heard the surging energy around his hand dissipate.

There was that smile. It mocked him from cheek to cheek. Out of the corner of her eye she watched him as she stepped toward the center of the kneeling Danger Kids. Inclining her head forward, she waited for a short moment and Anthony deactivated his crest. Each of them followed and one by one she felt the energy fueling their powers leave them.

'*Aaron get ready*,' thought Alex to them all. '*As soon as you see it, give it everything you've got.*'

'*See what?*' begged Aaron confused by Alex's request.

'*You'll know when you do and you'll hit her as hard as you can. Lightning-Fire and all*,' thought Alex happily.

"Last one," said Sorcea as she turned toward Dark Shadow, savoring her victory over the Danger Kids. "I applaud your ability to have your friends make the smart choice. It is a shame they have to follow such a weakling. How could you follow one who won't put up a fight?" Sorcea looked sharply at Aaron provoking him with a smirk.

Aaron grunted when he heard the words depart from her lips. In that moment he wanted to strike her down.

"Whenever you're ready," said Sorcea to Dark Shadow.

Alex knew she couldn't see his eyes through his shades, but the tears streaming down his face were there for her eyes to see. Her smile grew larger as she watched him cry. Touching his chest, Alex's hand rested on his crest.

Crystal's eyebrows moved up her head as wonder crept into her mind, wondering what Dark Shadow was doing. She was looking for the signal, but he never told her what it was.

"Anytime now," said Sorcea, unable to see the symbol on his crest.

'*Exactly what I was thinking*,' thought Alex to Crystal. He nodded his head up and down. Crystal was watching him with a confused look on her face. '*Now*,' he thought to her, his tone screaming with anxiety.

*Crunch!*

Crystal's elbow collided with Sorcea's ribs. Crystal heard her gasp for air as her grip loosened on her neck.

"Now!" Alex screamed to Aaron.

At the top of his lungs Aaron roared as he jumped from his knees onto his feet, his crest illuminated, activating as he rose. A jagged beam of Lightning-Fire zipped from the palm of his hand and slammed into Sorcea's chest, sending her careening into the double doors of City Hall.

Sorcea screamed at the top of her lungs as her backside hit the cold stone. She was more embarrassed than she was angry.

Anthony raced toward Crystal and grabbed her by the waist, lifting her off of the ground. Zipping around quickly Anthony stumbled over a cop's foot and lurched forward.

"Oh my god do you even know what you're doing," screamed Crystal, at the top of her lungs, taken over by the feeling of falling.

"Crap," said Anthony as he twisted and landed on his back, Crystal falling on top of him.

"At least you're a gentleman," she said as she quickly pulled herself off of him. She dusted herself off and extended her hand to him. "Crystal."

'Chrono," said Anthony taking her hand and shaking it. "Looks like I gotta go," said Anthony as he heard Sorcea's voice booming in the distance.

"You're all deceitful liars. Just as bad as the traitors who once took my king from his throne," said Sorcea rising and then levitating into the air. "I've tried to be forthright with you all. Yet, it seems you understand only understand force and power. Today I will teach you all that you have very little of both."

"Bring it on," said Mirely, levitating into the air, facing off with Sorcea.

"Take this." Kareem launched an assault, sending balls of fire toward Sorcea. Rapidly they flew at her, but she watched them as if they were moving at the pace of a turtle. Her frown scared him.

"Simni," whispered Sorcea and the first ball of fire dissipated before it reached her.

"I think that says you're out of the fight," said Ray waving his finger as he spoke.

"You think you can do better?" Kareem knew Ray would think that he could.

"Let me show ya scrub." Ray swung his hammer, quickly building up speed as he swung it with one hand. Kareem could hear it whistling in the wind, and Alex could feel the magnetic energy around it.

*Whoosh!*

Ray's hammered buzzed as he released it into the air. Magnetic energy guided it toward Sorcea, fast as a bullet. She remained composed. She watched the hammer as she had watched the balls of fire.

Reaching her hand toward the zooming hammer, she whispered a word. *"Stagganna."* The hammered stopped mid flight and dropped from the air, crashing into the stone steps below.

Air flew past Alex and he watched Ray grab Anthony by the collar before he fell forward, helping to right him.

"So what's the plan boss man?" asked Anthony of Alex, seeming cheerful. "Oh thanks," said Anthony in a matter of fact way to Ray as he landed on his heels.

"I'm trying to figure that out," said Alex watching Sorcea clap her hands together as if praying. He watched her eyes go completely black and saw illumination behind her shirt. A ringing slipped into his ear bothering him a bit. He watched Anthony hit the ground hard with his knees, grabbing at his ears. He managed to push the ringing out of his ears with his telekinesis. "No." He murmured to himself as he watched Mirely fall from the sky into Ray's waiting arm. Alex hadn't noticed him move toward her. He thanked God that Ray's reaction time was much better than his. Looking to his left he saw Aaron and Kareem writhing in pain on the ground. Behind him he could hear the cops and onlookers screaming in pain holding their ears.

Sorcea's throaty laugh echoed into the air around him. Ray was standing next to Alex, but he was occupied, holding Mirely who squirmed in his arms.

"What are we gonna do?" begged Alex to Ray.

"You're supposed to be the leader."

Suddenly Ray's helmet flew from his head and he collapsed in pain, with Mirely in his arms, his ears ringing with pain.

In a flash Sorcea was standing in front of Dark Shadow as the rest of the Danger Kids squirmed on the ground with everyone else.

"Bravery has gotten you no where."

"Fazzoms," he said shocked at how fast she moved.

Guh! Alex's neck hurt as he felt her hand close tightly around his throat. He couldn't think straight. His skull felt like it had been split open and his legs began to shake uncontrollably as he collapsed to his knees, hitting the ground hard.

"Reminds me of the first day we met," said Sorcea tightening the grip around Alex's neck until he began to suffocate. "You suffered on your knees then. Remember?"

Then he heard the voice in his head again. It wasn't angry with him. There was no sadness. Only an overwhelming feeling of disappointment registered in Alex's mind. He was a failure again. Yet it wasn't him who was thinking those thoughts. Someone else was there in his head. He thought it was Sorcea, but the voice was unmistakably male. There was no coming back from it, as its talk bashed his courage and quality as a leader. The voice hated him. At her hands he'd die first. That much, Sorcea had said before he could no longer hear and his eyelids closed.

# FOREVER KNOWN AS HEROES

Crystal watched in horror seeing Dark Shadow collapsing in Sorcea's grip. Police officers were scattered about the asphalt, holding their ears, yelling in pain. The service weapons they'd drawn on Sorcea lay on the ground close to them, no help to anyone. A few of the onlookers had gotten away, while the rest were on the ground in obvious pain.

Crystal was confounded, staring at hundreds of people on the ground suffereing under one woman's control. Even the Danger Kids, who she'd seen do impossible things we no better off. She remembered Dark Shadow saying they were the good guys. "Aren't the good guys supposed to save the day?"

She had no clue why she'd asked herself the question aloud. No one could hear her. She had to make an effort to hear herself. The ragged screams of pain made her cringe in fear as she watched people suffer.

Before she noticed, her hands were lifting her camera, the index finger of her right hand ready to press the shutter button. Then she thought of Jessica Duarte, the news reporter she wanted to be like. If she knew Jessica, she'd be right in the thick of it.

Crystal let go of her camera and looked at the last place she'd seen Jessica. She'd moved. They told her to get away. Her breathing became labored as she thought of Jessica leaving the scene of the juiciest story of the year. *No way she'd leave* Crystal thought. She must be in pain like everyone else.

"Ah!"

Crystal's shoulders tensed, moving closer to her neck as she lifted her hands bracing for impact. Her labored breaths became pants and tears welled in her eyes as fear gripped her by the heart, tearing out her courage. Never had she heard someone scream so loud. The pain must have been unbearable for the boy who could read her mind. She suffered with him from distance as she watched him holding Sorcea's forearm. His neck was craned back in an awful position that was sure to leave a crick in his neck if it remained that way long enough.

Then the question dawned on her. "Why am I not hurt? Why can't I hear what everyone else is hearing? Her hand hurt my neck for as long as she'd held it. Crazy dame, I ought to call the police…wait they're all down. That was dumb. Think. I am thinking aren't I? O-M-G!" The solution escaped her. What was she supposed to do? She couldn't read anyone's mind or throw lightning bolts from her hands, let alone fly. She was as helpless as she'd been before she was saved. "They saved me." The thought made her happy. Life. That was the one thing she had. She was alive and well. "Seems like everyone else is on their way out. I'm horrible. Think." She begged herself and kneeled down behind a car. Stroking her head, she pulled her hair back behind here ears.

The seconds she'd spent trying to formulate a perfect plan seemed like forever. She'd come up with nothing and frustration set in immediately, wrenching her nerves. A flash of light swung past her and she ducked lower. Creeping along the trunk of the car she watched it as it spun over the scene. It was blacker than anything she'd seen, but bright as the light of the moon.

"It's coming from her neck," she said to herself. Blinking her eyes fast, she wondered if that's what it was that was causing everyone pain.

Crystal remembered taking pictures of her at the park when the pandemonium ensued. It was the same woman taking on the same group of kids in costumes, now with an extra buddy, clad in shining metal armor. She could see sunlight glistening off the helm sitting next to him face down. "The power of prayer." Crystal had noticed Sorcea slap her hands together before everyone started dropping to the ground. The first time she'd seen her, she was dressed like a nun. Her clothes hadn't much chained, except there was no rosary or rope that symbolized her religious beliefs. All she was now was a mean freak dressed in black. Her robes were drawn back to her sides, split up the middle to her hip line, revealing tight black leather pants. She noticed that her boots had a sharp point, much like a witch. "That's appropriate I guess." As much as they were like a witch's boots, Crystal thought they were quite stylish. "Think about how to help dummy," she chastised herself and began to ramble her thoughts senselessly.

Slowly one of her favorite movies came to mind. It featured an actor that she thought was the dreamiest she'd ever seen. He portrayed a brutal warrior with a code of honor who was nothing like his real life self. But she remembered his words before the final battle against a tyrannical king, but spoke the thoughts her own mind had concocted. "Maybe I'll die a martyr and be beloved by everyone. Or they'll think I'm just some stupid little girl who should have been home with her mother." She stood up and slapped at her skirt, dusting it off, while hoping more to remove the wrinkles. "To think of it, my mother told me to come home right after school," she said turning toward Sorcea. Three steps more she took toward her. She pulled her hair back and wrapped it into a ponytail. "Oops...sorry." She'd clipped a police officer's forehead with her shoe as she stepped over him. He barely noticed, writhing in pain.

The street seemed wider than it actually was, and she wished it were, having made it more than halfway across. The throng of police cars, fallen police, news vans and citizens made the street seem bigger.

"Yeah she noticed." Terror gripped her, as Sorcea's gaze was casted upon her young face. Her heart pounded in her chest at the thought of what might happen next. The scowl on the mad witch's face expressed grinding teeth and deep measured breaths of incredulity. "Yeah the nerve I must have. The stupidity that must operate my brain, I know, even though I'm certainly one of the brightest lights under the lampshade; still I just take pictures and write lies in the school paper, filtered with a little bit of truth here and there. I must be mad to be doing this.

Gotta die sometime. Might as well be for a bunch of freaks in costumes that saved my life. What else is there to life but a great story?"

The words of that warrior ran through her mind again. Her heart pounded harder in her chest. She was sure her blood pressure had shot through the roof and she'd collapse in a few seconds. Sweat accumulated on her brow and she rubbed her palms with her fingers trying to dry them of perspiration.

Just a few more steps and she'd be face to face with her. "Too far to turn back now. Yeah, he said that in the movie. But, his muscles are a lot bigger than mine. He's so dreamy...uh snap out of it," she said disappointed in herself that she was thinking about a hunk faced with such danger. Yet, he was the one who had said it. He was the one who gave her the guts to be a reporter and chase any story like her idol Jessica Duarte who was probably knocked to the ground with everyone else. And then she said them quietly to herself. They gave her courage as she watched Sorcea let go of Dark Shadow's neck, letting him fall onto his back. "Those who stand up in times of great danger are forever known as heroes."

Crystal had never been one to stare. Her mother had taught her that it was rude. Yet, that's what she did. Deeply she stared into Sorcea's eye and waited, as eternity seemed to drift by.

Slowly, the lines of Sorcea's lips became tighter, as the frown on her face deepened. Her breathing became heavy, almost labored, as she stared at the girl. Why wasn't she hurt? Why wasn't she writhing in pain with everyone else? She had no power. Even the Danger Kids had fallen.

Sorcea screamed and the black light swung around faster. Crystal cringed in fear as the people, the police, and the Danger Kids suffered more in pain on the ground.

Shock registered on Sorcea's face as Crystal stood there motionless, staring at her.

Crystal shook her head *no* and tears welled in her eyes. Other than stand her ground, she couldn't figure out exactly what she was supposed to do next. There was nothing special about her as far as she was concerned. She was just a reporter. "Stop this." Somehow she found the courage to speak. Crystal blinked unsure of what to say next. But she didn't' have to think about it.

"Have you lost your mind?" asked Sorcea harshly.

"Yes, yes I have," said Crystal. "Only a crazy person would give up their life to save all these strangers. But they helped me, so here I am. I'll never win a Pulitzer, but there's always a camera somewhere. Somebody will tell my story. And I'll be famous still, just like Jessica Duarte." The pride she felt was enormous and her face wore a smile to match the feeling.

"So you want to be a hero then?" Sorcea's hand shot out and grasped Crystal by the top of her head.

The black light settled over top of them and the object behind Sorcea's shirt radiated faster. The magnificent black light covered everything and everyone around them, and the light from the sun was blotted out.

Crystal grabbed at Sorcea's wrist, trying to pry her hands away. She could feel her scalp fighting to keep her hair in tact.

Sorcea bore down on Crystal, her face directly over the young girl's. "Death is the inevitable end that all feeble creatures must suffer. Suffer yours today."

A beam of black light shot from the object behind Sorcea's shirt toward Crystal's face. Crystal gasped as she watched the dark matter fly toward her from the short distance away. It seemed to happen in slow motion. She could see each tiny increment the dark light traveled. Fear wanted her to close her eyes, but her courage wanted her to watch. If it were to be the end, she'd like to see it.

"Uh." Crystal turned her face slightly and gasped as the light touched her face. The light was magnificent, but it wasn't blinding like the sun. It wasn't cold, as she'd expected it to be, but warm and comforting. She felt like she was being cradled in the arms of her mother. Quickly her fear subsided and she smiled.

Slowly the dark light that enveloped Crystal's face began to creep toward her eyes and she felt the clutch on her hair no longer.

She could see plainly through the black light that had begun to enter into her eyes. She could see Sorcea as well, panic on her face as she reached toward a black crystal in the shape of a ragged crescent moon.

The object pulled at the necklace around Sorcea's neck. "No," cried Sorcea wrapping her hand around the crystal. Smoke began to seep out from the spaces in her fist. She cried out in pain as the gem began to burn her palm. As the black crystal began to sizzle Sorcea relented and released her grasp of it. The necklace suddenly snapped, leaving the gem suspended between Crystal and Sorcea.

The black light continued to poor into Crystal's eyes as the gem floated toward her. The pores on her skin began to tingle as the black energy filled her. Inside she could feel something change inside her, but she didn't feel as if she were being invaded.

The gem was warm when it touched the skin just below her collarbone. The warm crystal object dressed her in a black and purple costume, leaving her shoulders and back exposed. The black energy around her began to turn into a cloud-like mist with black particles floating around inside of it. As she moved her hand in front of her face, it was transparent, though still visible.

"This can't be happening," said Sorcea, breathing heavily. She was nearly frantic as she watched Crystal transform. Looking at her, she was reminded about the girl she'd read about in her ancestor's book. It had led her to the crystal-like gem she'd worn. She knew the tale well and Crystal's eyes had yet to turn completely black, but she could see the black dots on the veins in her eyes. That was the first sign. "You're back."

Crystal heard her and raised her eyebrows in confusion.

"Die!" Sorcea raised her hand and blasted a large beam of lightning-fire at Crystal.

Throwing her hands up in front of her chest, Crystal screamed. "Whoa!"

*Swoosh!*

The cloud-like mist around Crystal's hands swelled. The black particles floating around radiated quickly and began to swirl like a vortex.

The lightning fire boomed against the mist that began to trickle away from Crystal's hands. Then a sound like air being softly blown out emanated from the mist and the lightning fire was dragged into the black swirl.

The sucking sound was soft as the lightning fire was dragged into the swirl. Crystal could feel the force throughout her body and felt the energy tickling at every part of her skin. There was a rush of excitement inside of her as her heart pounded.

What she felt was exhilarating and she imagined it was the same feeling that people got when they went mad. Yet, her mind was at a standstill while her emotions seemed heightened. The small victory of avoiding the concussive force of the lightning-fire blast gave her even more confidence.

"Would you like to try that again?" Crystal spoke with pride. She wanted to test herself.

Sorcea entered into a rage and raised her hands above her head. "How dare you try to make a mockery of me you miserable little brat!" Crossing her wrists Sorcea began to chant quickly and a ball of green energy the size of a basketball formed. With a wave of her arms, Sorcea sent the ball of energy at Crystal.

Crystal's confidence rose again as she felt her skin prickle as the ball of energy raced toward her. Raising her hands quickly she stopped the rotating ball of energy and absorbed it again.

Suddenly Crystal felt her hands shaking and the clear cloud-like mist around her hand began to turn green and orange. She closed her hands into a fist and lightning began to radiate around her. The energy entered into a state of flux and she could feel it begging to be released.

Sorcea watched in horror. The black energy that she had used to subdue everyone began to spin faster. She watched Crytal's confident gaze turn into a large smile. She watched as her pupils turned black, and then her iris. As Crystal breathed harder, the veins in her eyes bulged more and the black dots upon them began to turn her sclera black.

Everyone upon the ground began to scream in more agony. Faster the black light spun, now emanating from Crystal and Sorcea cringed slightly, feeling the pain she had wrought upon the Danger Kids, police, and onlookers.

Screaming loud, Crystal punched her fist forward and released the energy upon Sorcea that had been meant for her.

*Bang!*

The energy blast landed with concussive force, sending Sorcea spiraling back through the doors of City Hall.

Sorcea shot out of City Hall like a rocket yelling at Crystal, "You haven't seen the last of me."

Crystal smiled bigger, enjoying her victory. As her joy rose, the black light spun faster. The painful screams became louder and she looked around confused. Immediately she noticed that the black light was coming from her. She hadn't noticed it before but the cloud-like mist covering her hands was all around her body, and flowing outward away from her.

She could feel her heart pounding fast, and her breathing was still rapid. The feeling of joy and exhilaration quickly began to feel like a caffeine rush. As much as her mind was in control, these new found powers were feeding off of her emotional state.

"Calm down Crystal, take it easy, you won, big deal. Focus please. You're hurting everyone. Get a grip, get a grip." Crystal spoke quietly, coaching herself. She clasped her hands together and began to breathe deeply. Fear gripped her for a moment and hot tears ran down her face.

A sucking sound raced around her and she could feel the black spinning light coming back toward her. She could hear people around her begin to stir and she wanted desperately to leave.

"I hope this works." Keeping the black light around herself and the Danger Kids, she pushed her mind toward Dark Shadow. "Take me to where you last were." It wasn't Dark Shadow's voice she heard but her own after making her demand. *'Read his thoughts. Say the word Magortis.'* *'Magortis,'* she said and the black light that had caused everyone so much pain spun like a vortex and pulled her and the Danger Kids inside of it.

"Welcome to Aqua Max." Crystal heard a familiar voice and then quickly looked up.

A look of astonishment painted her face. "Ms. Clark?"

# TOMORROW

Seeing Ms. Clark was a total shock for Crystal. She'd expected to have to ask some question and have them answered. Having them answered by a teacher she'd known of for as long as she'd been a student was an entirely different thing. Aqua Max was freaky enough on it's own, but she'd assumed it was where the Danger Kids met, planned, and launched their short list of missions to date. Every team of superheroes had one on television. How Ms. Clark played into it all would be an interesting story. That's at least what Crystal thought. She was at the very least comforted to see a familiar face.

"I'm sure you can probably guess that I have a few questions. My notepad and camera are here somewhere." Crystal touched the skintight get up she was wearing and wondered how her old outfit fit under it. "Hmmm," Crystal began, curling her lips in thought, "I always wondered what superheroes did with their other clothes. Trippy."

"Magical matter manipulation, quite a simple process," said Ms. Clark. She tried to maintain an air of confidence and calm, but her mind was stirring. Her eyes danced around Crystal like a mad scientist trying to solve the last problematic detail of their greatest invention.

"I guess that makes sense. But the thing is, how do I get these spandex off? It's not the most fashionable thing in the world. I certainly have an image to uphold." Crystal was incensed at the idea of remaining in her new black and purple get up for much longer. She longed for the looser garments she'd worn to school.

"Do you have a crest?" asked Ms. Clark curious.

"What's a crest?"

"A small spherical gem with a symbol etched into the surface," replied Ms. Clark interested.

"I had a little black crystal gemmy thing that dressed me up in tights. Made me go a little crazy for a moment, I was sure I was going to lose myself. But I had some fun, though I never want it to happen again. Plus, everyone was in pain and I kind of liked the feeling as much as it made me feel like I drank too many Red Bulls. And if-."

Crystal would have never stopped speaking if Ms. Clark hadn't cut her off. "Everyone was in pain?" Ms. Clark's forehead folded in contemplation, begging for the answer.

"Yes. Well, the crazy lady did it first and then the black light went inside me. Wait, weren't you watching? If not, what are all these screens for?" Crystal pointed to all of the monitors in the Aqua Max control room. Most of them were displaying the news, which was airing the very event the two were speaking of now.

"Of course, but after a certain point, everything was disrupted. There was tons of static on some channels. Others were completely blacked out," said Ms. Clark, her face still a mass of befuddlement. "How again did you get your powers?"

"When the crazy lady tried to attack me, the light went inside me."

"The black light?"

"Yes, are you listening?"

"This isn't happening," said Ms. Clark the memory of something she had read crept into her mind.

"What isn't happening...wait that's the same thing she said, what's going on?"

On the floor the Danger Kids began to stir, sitting up on the floor. Mirely rubbed the back of her neck, swinging her head toward each shoulder. Her neck cracked on the second swing, relieving the crick she'd felt after sitting up.

"We saved her," said Mirely, breathing a sigh of relief.

"I think it's the other way," said Crystal before she recognized the voice of her cousin. Her eyes went wide with excitement, fear, and then confusion. "You're a Danger Kid?" Crystal marched toward Mirely excited seeing through the pixie dust glamour to disguise her face. "I can't believe you didn't tell me. How could you? I'm your cousin, and like your only cousin that really matters."

"I couldn't," said Mirely being mashed into Crystal's chest as her cousin wrapped her arms around her, smashing her arms against her rib cage.

"We all had to keep it a secret," said Alex as he pulled his shades off.

"No way," said Crystal as she noticed her other friends. She was smiling from ear to ear. She hugged each one of them tightly and came to Ray and stuck her hand out. "We're not on hugging terms yet." She smiled bigger and squeezed her palms together under her chin. "This is really good. I wont be the only freak among my friends. No Clark Kent issues here."

"We'll hug at a later date." Ray shook hands tightly with Crystal.

"Firm grip," she replied.

"How dare you define one of the greatest superheroes of all time as a freak," said Alex taken aback at the insult directed at his favorite hero of all time.

"Whatever," replied Crystal and turned back to Ms. Clark. "Now that I know the Danger Kids are my friends. Well most of them." She rolled her eyes at Aaron. "Can you tell me about what isn't happening about me?"

"Huh," said Anthony confused.

"My powers," replied Crystal.

"You have powers?" said Anthony shocked.

"Duh pencil neck, why do you think she called herself a freak," said Aarron popping Anthony on the back of the head.

*Smack!*

"And how do you think we got here," asked Kareem. "Sometimes I wonder if you have a brain in your head at all."

"Oh yeah right...yeah...hmm." Anthony leaned against a chair and fiddled with his fingers. "One question."

"Hold on to it." Mirely pressed her forefinger against his lips. "Is there something wrong Ms. Clark?" Mirely was concerned. She could read the tone of Crystal's question.

"There's something about Crystal's powers that I fear could put her in danger. If I am right, the entire city could be at risk."

"Fazzoms?" Alex grew anxious. "I thought Dorigon was a threat to the entire city."

"Dorigon wants to rule again. Crystal could very well destroy us all."

"How is this possible?" said Mirely. She was more afraid than Alex was. Her eyes welled with tears as she looked at Crystal who seemed to be floored by the news.

"A danger to myself." The words floated out her mouth, barely louder than a whisper. "These powers helped me save everyone."

"But you also hurt them too," said Ms. Clark fast. She didn't want to give Crystal any time to form any logic around her accomplishment.

"This superhero nonsense keeps getting better and better," said Kareem shaking his head *no*. "One thing's for sure Alex, you're still the worst of us."

Crystal smiled at Kareem and he stepped closer to Alex.

"At least I'm not afraid of girls," said Alex whispering to Kareem.

"Shut up." Kareem nudged Alex in the side with his elbow.

"I need to do some digging," said Ms. Clark walking toward Crystal. "Give me your hands."

Crystal placed her hands in Ms. Clark's hands. Crystal closed her eyes after being instructed to do so.

"Imagine yourself as you were before and think the words *revesti ef'iagi*."

Crystal thought the words and felt her pores open and the black light that had filled her slipping away, reforming the crystal in front of her. As the crystal became whole again, she looked at her arms and noticed that there was small black dots lining her arms that slowly disappeared.

"What is it?" begged Crystal with great worry.

"Don't worry about it now," said Ms. Clark, inclining her head toward Crystal's arms so she could see that the black spots were no longer visible.

The gem bobbed there in the air between them and Ms. Clark said, "Hmm. Let me guess." Reaching up, she touched the crystal and felt it began to get warm. The black light began to emanate and she could feel the heat radiating around it. "Take it."

Crystal reached out and took the crystal from the air. Looking at it, it dazzled her like a diamond wedding ring. "It'll hurt everyone else wont it?"

Ms. Clark gave her a halfhearted attempt at a smile. "You've guessed right. Before you made contact with the crystal, anyone could have taken it and used it's power. Now that's it's found you, it will never let you go." Speaking the word *trecase*, a clasp and chain appeared in Ms. Clark's palm. She handed it to Crystal sullenly.

Crystal slipped the crystal into the clasp and slipped the chain on her neck.

"Keep it out of sight and don't use it," said Ms. Clark moving her toward the Danger Kids.

"I have question," said Crystal hotly.

"They'll have to wait until tomorrow."

"What, no. I have to know what this thing might do to me," said Crystal.

"Your mother will also want to know where you have been, especially after today. It is nearly five-thirty. You all need to get home." Ms. Clark ushered them into a circle and they joined hands. "You all know the words. I'll see you tomorrow."

# A HUNDRED WORLDS AWAY

How Ms. Clark managed to find a reasonable way to work them all into detention again was beyond Kareem. He wished Brick were with them. In Kareem's mind, Brick was more to blame for the outburst that created the commotion that drove Ms. Clark to give them detention. He rubbed his forehead with the tips of his fingers, agitated about losing another logic contest with Ms. Clark. She gave him no way to weasel his way out of an extra homework assignment. Ray challenged her as he had before, but in Kareem's mind, Ray seemed to more so be securing his seat in detention, rather than truly being opposed to Ms. Clark. As much as that might have been true, his logic was a lot better than Kareem's. Not to mention, he had the uncanny ability of finishing his class work before anyone except Mirely.

Mirely was an entirely different animal. Despite the fact that Crystal seemed to be more powerful than all of them, she was still the bravest. Where she found the courage he was unsure. She'd been a certified cupcake all of her life. They're family he thought to himself, curling his lips annoyed.

Looking over at Alex, Kareem rolled his eyes, watching his best friend work diligently on finishing his assignment. Alex seemed not to have a care in the world, leaning his head against his closed fist. "Nothing like having a best friend who doesn't help you." Kareem made sure to be quiet enough not to rouse Ms. Clark's attention, but loud enough for Alex to hear him, as he tapped his pencil against a sheet of paper.

"Giving you answers, and helping you are two entirely different things," said Alex softly.

'It's helping me if you give me the answers." Looking around, Kareem noticed that everyone else was as relaxed as Alex seemed to be. Even Anthony seemed unfazed about detention. Then again, nothing ever fazed Anthony. "How does that dope always seem to be so cool about everything?"

"Who?" inquired Alex.

"Anthony, look at him."

Alex turned his head slightly to find Anthony whistling quietly to himself, while twiddling with an action figure. He wore a soft smile on his face, his eyeballs moving about as his mind worked.

"Maybe he's figured it out like the rest of us." Alex faced Kareem as he said it, seeing a confused stare on his buddy's face.

"Worked out what?"

"That we're not in detention because we're in any real trouble."

"Then why are we having it if we're not. I want to go outside." Kareem began to lean in closer to Alex so that he could hear him clearly. The volume of his words would have gone up if he hadn't. "I want to play, I want to look at girls as they walk away to the school bus, and whistle at them like dirty plumbers and construction workers. I'm trapped. Okay, I'm trapped." His voice squeaked as sat upright. His body vibrated and he jerked his shoulders back as Ms. Clark's eye caught him as he stilled himself.

"Have you ever guessed that maybe we're in detention in order to have a reason to tell our parents why we never get home right after school." Alex noticed that Kareem gave him a funny look. "More importantly to learn how to use our powers."

"Duh, I knew that," said Kareem with a smile. "I just wanted to see if you knew."

Crystal walked through the door of Ms. Clark's room twenty minutes after the Danger Kids' detention began. Crystal gave everyone a twiddled-finger wave, wearing a large smile on her face. Stepping deeper into the room, she leaned over Ms. Clark's desk to see what she was doing. She found the small woman reading an old dusty book that looked too heavy for her to carry.

"Close the door please," said Ms. Clark without raising her eyes toward Crystal.

"Sure thing," said Crystal, shuffling swiftly to the door, shutting it with a bang.

"Was that entirely necessary?" asked Ms. Clark.

"I'm charged up."

"You're late. I told you to be here at the sounding of the final bell."

"And you're not my teacher, and I'm editor of the school paper, and the article for the "Fall Into Winter Dance" was never done by Mr. Elmwood here. Then I had to post one hundred fifty flyers around school. If I didn't have David Seddon to help me I'd still be out there. I like David. He's smart. He's reliable. Most importantly, he knows Batman's a far better super hero than Superman."

"Total stab," said Kareem smiling wide from ear to ear. He could hear Alex breathing in deeply wanting to argue. "I love you." The words came out with a sound fainter than a whisper. He'd never let her hear it.

"Do you always ramble?" asked Ms. Clark standing up, leaning toward Crystal, her palms firmly planted on her desk.

"I don't ramble, I get my point across using every word necessary available to me in the English language. I like to be prim so there's no misinterpretation Ms. Clark. Wouldn't want anyone to think I didn't want his article on time," said Crystal rolling her eyes at Alex.

"Work out your periodical issues on your on time. You're treading on mine." Ms. Clark's voice was stern, almost combative.

"I'll try."

"You'll try?" Ms. Clark raised her eyes brows in shock.

"I'm a busy girl. People rely on me."

"I rely on you to be on time or else. Come!" Ms. Clark barked the last word and everyone stood up and moved to the front of the room close to her desk. "Hands."

"A little short on words today Ms. Clark," said Ray with his usual sarcasm.

"Very," she replied and lifted a hand toward her desk. The old book floated toward her and then rested softly on her palm.

"Looks heavy," said Ray.

"It's not," shot Ms. Clark. '*Magortis.*'

The ride through the portal was fast. It felt like they were yanked hard and abruptly pushed to a stop. The familiar white walls and glass windows rose around them almost immediately as Max welcomed them in his kind computerized voice.

Seven white chairs rose up out of the floor, facing the center screen. Each of the Danger Kids sat down and Ms. Clark stood in front of them. The book on Ms. Clark's palm floated away from her and bobbed in the air. The pages began to turn fast. Near the end of the book, the pages began to slow and then stopped and turned to face the Danger Kids.

Ms. Clark took in a deep breath and then began to speak. "Before my ancestor Felix Mysticgo created the Danger Kids crests, he created another one. The crest gave the wearer considerable power, nearly rivaling his own. The raw power of the crest allowed its wearer to do amazing and terrible, terrible things. Mysticgo took comfort in knowing that when he was gone someday, that there'd be a power in Atlantis greater than Dorigon's. While he favored Dorigon, he knew of the young prince's desires. He also knew of how strong he had become. For a year or so, the wearer of the crest was never needed, never tested in battle, but always taught. Taught to harness the power of the crest, to control it, and to control her emotional state. For a time the wearer succeeded. It wasn't until Dorigon's first act of defiance that all of Mysticgo's work had failed. Stop Dorigon she did, but in doing so unleashed a force of energy far greater than even Mysticgo could have imagined. With but a thought she subdued the whole of Atlantis, bringing them to their knees in splintering pain and agony. Only Mysticgo could stand against her. And so he did, calling upon his great power to subdue the girl he had given incredible power."

The Danger Kids looked on in astonishment and fear as Ms. Clark spoke. Their breaths were deep and long and their hearts beat fast. Ms. Clark knew they wanted to speak, to ask questions, but she continued uninterrupted.

"Mysticgo fought with the girl and each time it seemed that he had gained the upper hand, she would find new strength. The black light of the gem would push itself out, gathering more power. Feeling her strength rising, Mysticgo dug deep and pushed himself past the limits of his powers. The force that drove his powers filled him and at once, aged him and pulled at his life force. But his efforts had worked and he was stronger than the girl. It would seem that she would succumb to his might, but the gem that he used to create her crest did something he did not expect. When the girl felt his power, she too called upon the power of the gem to aid her. Enraged and angered at what she said was Mysticgo's betrayal, her true nature revealed itself. She was not pure of heart, as he had believed. She had no compassion for the weak and felt deep disdain for the royal family. All that she wanted was to rule. She wanted to take the throne of Atlantis for herself. The gem had driven her to madness. It fed off of her will to do harm and forced her deeper to that end. And the agonizing screams of the Atlantians made her happy.

When Mysticgo thought that she was vulnerable he attacked her with all of his might. Feeling the massive force generated by Mysticgo, the black light pushed itself out of the Earth's atmosphere. By Mysticgo's account, it drew energy from a hundred worlds away. It filled the girl with unimaginable power. Mysticgo had believed he'd die that day. But as she looked to use her newfound strength to destroy him, it killed her. The black light decimated her completely and all that was left was the black gem around Crystal's neck."

Crystal's eyes welled with tears slowly and then two lines of tears rolled down her cheeks. Ms. Clark wet her lips and began to walk but stopped short of taking a step. "The power you wield does not belong here," said Ms. Clark woefully. "However, there is a sad truth to this gem."

"What might that be?" said Kareem fearfully.

"The gem will not be had by anyone until you die or until it is returned to where it came from. There are only a few who could take it from you and they are-."

"A hundred worlds away," said Anthony, happy about finishing Ms. Clark's sentence as he interrupted her.

"So what am I supposed to do?" asked Crystal.

"Never use this power again," said Ms. Clark rapidly.

"Where does it come from?" begged Alex interested.

"Didn't you hear, a hundred worlds away," said Kareem, offering Alex the same annoyed look that he had given him earlier.

"A place called..." As Ms. Clark began to speak a buzzing alarm went off and red lights began to strobe about the chamber.

Max's voice erupted inside the chamber. "Alert, alert, there has been a breach, alert, alert."

Water began to poor into the chamber from behind them where the training room was and then a loud bang resounded against the door. A disgusted, ferociously scratchy voice yelled at them in Atlantian. The door boomed again and the string of Atlantian words erupted again with more anger and fervor.

*Woosh!*

A rapid jet of water pushed through half of the door after another loud boom. A massive foot entered into the chamber and a large hand pushed the door opened more, allowing the large man to step through.

"Dorigon," said Ms. Clark with fear as the Danger Kids began to back up to where Ms. Clark was standing. "Prepare yourselves."

*"Novus Fatum!"* Dorigon screamed Danger Kids with rage in his Atlantian tongue, his fists balled in furious rage. *Boom!* He slammed his fist into the door, pushing the bent door back into the frame, slowing the incoming water to a crawl. *'Ja wa keis shing.'*

# ULTIMATUM

The room grew silent as Dorigon began to stroll slowly toward them. He wore an expression of confidence and ill will. He hulked over everyone in the room, including Ray, who was tall for his age. Midway through his stride he stopped and clasped his hands behind his back and took a deep breath. His eyes fell on Ms. Clark and his lips twitched as if he'd begin to speak. Only his eyebrows and neck moved here and there, the lines on his forehead wrinkling. Ms. Clark's face moved and twisted and her forehead filled with lines.

Dorigon and Ms. Clark stood there for a tense moment, staring at one another. The expressions on their face informed that they were communicating. Time seemed to stand still for the Danger Kids who watched them both intently. Alex had tried infiltrating their minds so that he might hear, but felt a powerful psychic barrier each time he did. He realized that it was not Ms. Clark keeping him out, but Dorigon alone. Her barrier was strong, but he'd never felt a force push against his mind the way Dorigon's did.

Fear pumped blood through Alex's body, his heart beating rapidly. He wondered what he'd be able to do against Dorigon if he used his mind against him.

"What are we gonna do?" Aaron whispered to Alex.

Mirely shushed him, her eyes darting from Aaron to Dorigon and then back to Ms. Clark as she studied their expressions.

Dorigon laughed softly, his shoulders rising and falling, and then slowly his mouth began to open as he titled back his head. "Perhaps I should speak in this foolish drivel you call a language and allow these Danger Kids to decide their fate." His voice was full of bass, harsh, scratching and gurgling as he spoke. "I can feel your fear."

Alex looked around at everyone as the words slipped from Dorigon's lips. He could only have been talking to him alone. He could feel his heart beating inside his chest. At some points he thought he could hear it. Everyone's face was covered except Crystal and Mirely's so he couldn't read fear on anyone's expression. Ms. Clark seemed like a cold stone statue, standing and waiting for whatever might happen. *You are a coward.* Alex heard the words in his head and closed his eyes, turning his head to one side trying to quiet his mind.

"You are children, and I see no need to kill you. You may hand over your crests and I shall spirit you away to the safety of your homes. Or, you may deny my request and stand against me in a futile attempt to save yourselves and the miserable weaklings you have defended against Sorcea. Do this and I will make you suffer." Dorigon surveyed the Danger Kids for a moment as no answer came as he'd expected it to. He wasn't use to long pauses in conversation.

"How about this," said Ray stepping forward, clutching his hammer. "Take your ultimatum and shove it." As Ray spoke the words *shove it*, he spun and cracked Dorigon across the face with his hammer, sending his flying backward into the door he'd come through.

Dorigon stood slowly; peeling himself out of the dent his body had put in the door. He smiled softly, looking at Ray almost as if in pleasure. *"Ja wa hing keis'ang shing."* Dorigon spoke in a harsh whisper as his dark burgundy eyes began to glow. A cold gust of air swept through the chamber, swirling around Dorigon as his hands were covered with burgundy energy.

"Ready yourselves Danger Kids," said Ms. Clark as her own eyes began to glow.

The gem on Crystal's neck began glowing and the black gem around her neck began to dance. A frown dressed Crystal's face as her clothing began to change. Purple leggings began rising up her legs and her torso became dressed in black. She screamed at the top of her lungs and a wave of black speckled misty energy burst from her hand.

Dorigon responded as the beam of energy raced toward him, pressing his hand forward and shooting his own beam.

*Kaboom!*

A shockwave burst from the collision of their energy pushing everyone back across the room. Ms. Clark found her backside against the control panel, nearly folding over backward.

"No Crystal!" Ms. Clark yelled, reaching her hand out toward Crystal. "You mustn't," said Ms. Clark crying out *'Magortis dusive've!'* Crystal vanished in a black cloud of smoke.

Mirely gasped seeing Crystal disappear from her sight. Again she gasped as Dorigon's energy slammed against the control module behind Ms. Clark, cracking it, and knocking pieces onto the floor.

Ray turned again and threw his hammer with all of his might, grunting all the while.

"Not this time runt," said Dorigon of the largest Danger Kid as he caught the hammer in flight, turning as he did and sent it rocketing back toward Ray.

*Clank! Boom!* The ringing of metal on metal reverberated around the room as Ray grunted, feeling the shock of his own hammer banging into his armor.

In a flash, Dorigon ran toward him, as Ray grabbed the handle of his hammer. Ray raised his hammer to swing and suddenly screamed, "Whoa!" feeling a gust of wind that couldn't have come from outside. He heard Dorigon grunt and watched him spin into the air like a cyclone after Anthony struck him with a double fisted punch. Another gust of air whipped past Ray, and he blinked fast under his helmet, shocked at the incredible speed and power Anthony had just displayed.

Then Ray heard Anthony yell, "Not again," as he watched him tumble into the edge of the control panel. "Uh." Anthony grabbed at the control panel and pulled himself up.

"No way," said Aaron as he watched Dorigon slow himself, spin the opposite way out of the air and shoot back onto the floor. He closed the distance in a flash, grabbing Anthony by the back of the head. Dorigon banged the boy's against the panel, knocking him unconscious.

"No," screamed Mirely as she rose into the air, wind swirling around her. Her arms were opened wide and her face held an angry scowl. Her hands illuminated as she cast her gaze upon Dorigon. A rush of water shot toward him from Mirely's hands.

"Do you wish to soak me to death?" said Dorigon with a smirk, allowing the rushing water to slam into his chest. It drove him back two short steps and he began to mock Mirely with a throaty laugh.

Aaron whipped a bolt of lighting toward Dorigon as his head rolled back in laughter. It crackled and popped as it struck him, evaporating the water as it sent shockwaves through his body.

"Uhhh!" Dorigon screamed loud falling to one knee and looking up.

"Don't stop," said Ms. Clark imploring the Danger Kids to continue their assault. She raised one hand and whipped it toward him, sending out a beam of energy in the form of a rope. Then again she did it, allowing the energy to wrap around Dorigon's wrists.

Dorigon pulled his hands toward his chest as he rested on one knee, trying to drag Ms. Clark toward him. "What?" He said quietly to himself as he heard her mumbling a spell. He tried to focus his hearing so that he could discern the words she was speaking. "Uh." He gasped, feeling the ropes stretched his arms backward, pulling at his chest. He grunted again and felt a ball of fire smash against him.

"Take that hot shot," said Kareem bouncing up and down as he threw balls of fire at Dorigon.

Dorigon's eyes began to glow and a force field rose up around him. The balls of fire Kareem was throwing began to dissipate as they collided with the force field.

"Everyone at once," screamed Ms. Clark. "It's the only way to break his barrier. He'll only be able to hold up for so long."

Ray grabbed his hammer and righted himself and began banging away at Dorigon's force field. "Don't mind me, or do," said Ray to Dorigon as he swung harder and faster, spinning as he banged away at Dorigon's force field.

Mirely screamed and blasted Dorigon's force field with water. Tears streamed down her eyes and soon waves formed from her hands, slamming hard against the barrier. Aaron quickly joined in, keeping two lightning bolts seemingly attached to the barrier. He breathed in deep and then out hard. Each time the bolts seemed to reinforce themselves, sending shockwaves through the force field that erupted and crackled harder each time a wave of water hit.

"Set a fire under his barrier," said Ms. Clark to Kareem.

"You're the wood, we're at camp, and all we need's a little fire." The smile on Kareem's face was full of pride. He stuck out his chest as his visor flashed orange, and a blaze of hot orange fire formed under Dorigon's barrier.

A scowl twisted the lower half of Dorigon's face as he felt the heat rise under the barrier shielding him for the Danger Kids' assault.

Alex stared, stuck in place, wondering what he should do. He had no energy projectiles to fire at Dorigon. He couldn't create magic energy ropes, or call forth a rain. He felt helpless. He'd no clue what to do.

"Use your mind to pull his barrier apart," screamed Ms. Clark to Alex, reading the confusion in his mind.

Alex closed his eyes and focused his mind. When he raised his hands toward Dorigon, he felt a wave of invisible energy push forward, pressing up against the barrier. He gasped, shocked at his ability. His eyes darted from one side to the other in shock. He locked eyes with Ms. Clark for a moment, as he marveled at the control he had. She spoke to him telepathically and told him to remain calm.

Dorigon screamed as she instructed Alex. Anger swelled up inside him. He feared being bested again by the Danger Kids. Closing his eyes he began to whisper to himself, the force field around him slowly weakening as the Danger Kids worked their magic.

"Just a little bit more," said Ms. Clark with a faint smile on her face. "His barrier is weakening." Then suddenly Ms. Clark felt her back split open, as a sharp object cut through her insides, and then her stomach was split open. She screamed in agony as she fell to her knees. The magical ropes around Dorigon's arms dissipated as she clutched at the open would in her belly.

Mirely screamed in horror first and then Alex, reaching out and stumbling forward slighting. The head of Ray's hammer slipped from his grasp and banged against the floor, the metal singing quietly. Kareem and Aaron stood with hands still outstretched, but their powers had subsided, as they stood motionless. Anthony had just begun to stir and when he turned he saw everyone standing dumbstruck and shook his head to clear it.

And then with his owns eyes Anthony saw the woman in black they'd first encountered leaning over Ms. Clark's right shoulder with half of her arm in his teacher's back. A blade of energy was sticking out of Ms. Clark's belly, and her middle and ring fingers were wrapped around it, touching the wound.

He watched her blood pour from the wound and his horror was compounded, as he saw a thin river of blood dripping from her blood soaked lips.

As he rose to his feet, freed from Ms. Clark's grasp, he spoke in Atlantian to his trusted minion. *'Sorcea, shing ga'ah preyvon shong sefi lowha've.'*

*'Ta emmi Ka, Ja shing gae'ehya ly,"* said Sorcea with a wicked smile on her face, happy to know that she had proven her loyalty to Dorigon.

"As for you," said Dorigon turning to Ray, "you shall suffer a far worse fate than this one here." He pointed at Ms. Clark as he mentioned her and then a bolt of energy knocked a grief stricken Mirely from the air, sending her slamming into the floor, unconscious.

Ray screamed and grabbed his hammer, but quickly suffered the same fate. Before Kareeem or Aaron could move, their heads were slammed together and the two crumbled to their knees, knocking into one another as they fell to the floor asleep.

"Not fast enough," said Dorigon with a treacherous smile as he caught a buzzing Anthony by the throat, lifting him from the floor. "Sleep now boy." Anthony tried to fight but his eyes soon rolled back as Dorigon squeezed tight the arteries in his neck, cutting off the blood flow to his brain.

He marched Anthony toward a quivering Alex who stood motionless, with tears running down the sides of his face. His shades hid red watery eyes as he fell to his knees.

Dorigon tossed Anthony to the side and continued to approach Alex. "You too will fail if you try to put up a fight. I gave you a choice and your master has suffered the consequences of the wrong decision. I speak to you in your foul tongue so that you might understand the gravity of the moment. She will die. This much is inevitable. But I am a kind and merciful king and shall spare you and your friends the misery of death. Surrender to me, by falling to your knees."

Alex shuddered and the voice in his head reminded him of all his fears. It beseeched him to surrender so that he might survive. The voice spoke OF all of his weaknesses to him clearly. He was made aware of them all again in that moment. He cried harder and the memories of all his past failures marched to the forefront of his mind. He'd quaked in fear in the park. His friends had bested him at every turn in the training room. And if they had all failed, there was nothing he could do. "It took all of us, including Ms. Clark, to even stand a chance against you." He had wanted to whisper it but it came out. Alex was ashamed of himself for saying it. Yet, he couldn't escape the truth of his words, no matter how much he wanted to. He wanted nothing more than to fold into himself.

"You cannot win." Dorigon said the words coolly.

"I can't win," said Alex crying harder as he fell to his knees.

Dorigon smiled in victory as he placed a hand against Alex's cheek and spoke in Atlantian, 'Sep ni sren,' and Alex fell asleep and fell into Dorigon's awaiting arms.

Dorigon held Alex to his chest like a loving parent and turned his head to Sorcea with a king's authoritative gaze. 'Faanis ehya ayn pripis ta res l'odeys.'

"She shall die, Emmi Ka," said Sorcea, hoping that somehow all of the sleeping Danger Kids could hear her.

'Margotis,' said Dorigon, and all of the Danger Kids were spirited away with him.

# HAVE MERCY

The first time she'd travel by teleportation Crystal thought that it was the most exhilarating experience of her life. Being thrust through time at space at a speed she wasn't willing to calculate was fun. The way from one point to another was like a subway station. It was dark, but a lit by random flashes of light. Only the light around her wasn't stuck against a wall of stone where mice crept quietly below. It was full of bustling energy; making swooshing sounds as the energy of the Margortis spell pushed her through.

How the word had come to her was a mystery when she spirited the Danger Kids from the throng of spectacle, after taking down Sorcea. It had tickled at her tongue for a split second, before she uttered the word.

For what seemed like an eternity she uttered the word a thousand times, but nothing happened. Within the grasp of Ms. Clark's spell she'd spun and twisted out of control. She had no true grasp of time or sense of direction. Unlike the usual straight-shot tunnel produced by uttering the word Margortis, Crystal felt as if she were being transferred from one tornado to another.

Every attempt she made at using the Margortis spell between each transfer only pushed her deeper into another vortex.

As time stretched on she had given up any attempts to use the Margortis spell to remove herself from her current predicament. She found herself unable to focus. She wondered what she could do to free herself. That's all she'd thought about for the entire time. Her heart pounded in her chest, as she wondered what was happening.

Deep down she didn't believe that she was a danger to the world. And even if she were, she'd rather take the chance to help. Being trapped did not suit her well. She hated being controlled and she hated being told what to do.

Looking down at the glowing gem around her neck she scoffed. "If this power is so great, why can't it get me out of this."

Crystal sucked in air, trying to reign in her disappointment. "What is the reverse of *Margortis*?" She asked herself the question and nibbled at her bottom lip. She spoke the word Margortis a dozen times quietly to herself. As she spoke the words, she begged her heart for it's meaning. Nothing happened and she continued the process until her mind quieted.

"*Margortis* means through time, through space," she said happily to herself aloud. Her skin became lined with goose bumps and she shuddered at an intense pressure crawling up her back. The words came from somewhere, but she could not hear a voice, though they surely hadn't originated from inside her. "I can't be going crazy, this is already crazy enough."

Then she thought harder, remembering that she had heard Ms. Clark speak a second word. "Uh!" She screamed, as she was jolted into another vortex.

Her body cartwheeled and then rotated forwards and backward, and then she wound like a screw, tumbling down a flight of stairs. "The word."

Closing her eyes she could see herself walking through the events as if they were happening again. First she saw Dorigon burst through the door and then she saw herself. She listened to Ms. Clark tell them all to ready themselves, and then she heard her. "*Dusive've*," she said aloud and then quickly the meaning came to her. "Infinitely."

The smile on her face was big. Her eyes rolled up in her head as she laughed at herself. "That's just perfect Ms. Clark, just perfect. I guess I'm supposed to just rot here."

Closing her eyes again, Crystal interlocked her fingers and took in a deep breath. She decided that she'd let the power of the spell take her wherever it wanted to. Forcing back the tension she was feeling, she allowed her shoulders to sink, as she placed her interlocked palms on her belly.

Slowly, Crystal began to stop tumbling and began to simply drift, as if she were being pushed down a flat sliding board. As she rested, her mind began to work at how she'd free herself. The black light burst into the black vortex, illuminating it more. The gem on her neck sung a song to her and the truth of her predicament slowly began to reveal itself to her.

"It was a protection spell," mouthed Crystal. "The reverse to the spell takes two days from within the Dusive spell." Crystal thought to herself sarcastically that needing to break the spell in two days was just great. "If I went missing for two days, my mother would have a coronary."

Unexpectedly, she felt something sharp press against her back and through her belly. She gasped at the pain, cringing as she floated into a seated position and began to roll. The force of the invasion knocked the wind from her and she reached at her stomach, expecting to find blood, but there was none.

Then, as if her sight had been blinded, the eight vortexes came into view and began to converge on one another. With great force, she felt herself being pushed to the center of the converging masses of energy and soon, she was suspended, face down in the tunnel of blackness she had expected to find herself the first time that she had said Margortis.

Crystal felt as if the tunnel exploded from behind her. The sound of the force that pushed her was akin to a thousand car engines being turned on at once. Crystal gasped softly as she was catapulted through the portal.

Sorcea pulled the energy blade from Ms. Clark's back and stood over her as she watched her collapse face first onto the floor. Ms. Clark began to crawl, trying desperately to drag herself away from Sorcea.

"Oh no, Mystic, you will not take the satisfaction from me. I will hear you beg for you life," said Sorcea viciously as she strolled behind Ms. Clark, grabbing her by the hair.

Sorcea turned Ms. Clark over onto her back and pressed her boot into her throat. Ms. Clark grabbed feebly at Sorcea's boot, trying to push the black shoe from her throat, but she was barely able to nudge it.

Reaching up with one hand, palm facing Sorcea, a rush of energy shot up, popping Sorcea in the face. Sorcea's head whipped slightly to one side. Her face snapped back, looking sharply at Ms. Clark, she scowled hard, and then pressed her boot more firmly against her throat.

"I guess you are where those brats get their stubbornness from." Sorcea balled up her fist and a thin line of energy formed at the small space between her fingers and palm. The energy was thin like the blade of an ice pick. With a flick her wrist, the energy sunk into Ms. Clark's shoulder, pressing it firmly to the floor. Another energy-pick went into Ms. Clark's other arm, holding her firmly in place against the floor.

"Killing me won't bring you what you want," said Ms. Clark weakly.

"But it'll bring me the satisfaction of knowing that I was always better," said Sorcea will ferocious anger.

Sorcea planted energy picks in Ms. Clark's hands and on both sides of her waist. Ms. Clark writhed in pain, hoping to free herself, but her energy was spent. Blood stained the white floors of Aqua Max and in that moment she wondered about the fate of the Danger Kids.

Ms. Clark knew that Dorigon would be far more merciless than Sorcea. Once he got what he wanted, he would give them no quarter. As much as he preached the delivery of mercy, she knew better than to believe it. All the things written about him in her ancestors' book said he was ruthless and satisfied his own whims.

"He will never love you. He will never trust you, and one day he shall do away with you when he has no more use for you." Ms. Clark sighed hard. It was as if she could feel life running away from her.

"My king has ordered me to kill you and I shall do just that," barked Sorcea with an ugly scowl.

Sorcea raised her hands and a ball of kinetic energy formed between them. "Goodbye Mystic," she said softly as she brought the ball of energy down.

*Swoosh!*

Shock and fear registered on Sorcea's face and she felt her hand being squeezed. The bones in her hands crackled as her knuckles and joints popped. She knew that her bones would soon break. The black light from the gem she once wore whipped around the room like the light from a flashing police car.

"Not what you were expecting?" said Crystal as she spun and flung Sorcea across the room. Sorcea crashed into the floor on her side. "It took me sometime to work it out, but what happened to her I could feel." Looking at Sorcea, Crystal could see the fear in Sorcea's eyes as she clawed her way to her feet. "Your actions broke the spell that brought me back here. I think I shall return the favor. But not before I make you suffer."

Tears rolled down Crystal's cheeks as the whole of her eyes turned completely black. She could feel Ms. Clark's life force slipping away through her own body, where Ms. Clark's wound was. Her black-misted energy swirled around her entire body, and the light swirling around the room returned to the gem around her neck, darkening it. Aqua Max began to shake as Crystal's power surged.

Feebly, Crystal could hear Ms. Clark say, "Please, you cannot," but she ignored her warning.

Turning her head slightly and looking over her shoulder, Crystal offered Ms. Clark a faint smile as her tears rolled. "You keep forgetting that you're not my teacher."

'*Margor-*' Sorcea tried to utter the word for the teleportation spell, but found her mouth unable to move.

'*Secessa*,' said Crystal before she could finish and began marching toward Sorcea.

Ten bolts of lightning whipped at Crystal in swift succession as she walked toward Sorcea. Her hands were moving rapidly as she swung wildly, hoping to floor Crystal before she got close enough, but the bolts simply bounced off of the aura surrounding her body.

As she grew closer, Sorcea levitated into the air and began circling, still throwing crackling bolts of lightning Crystal's way.

"Haven't you noticed by now that it's not going to work?" Crystal raised a hand toward Sorcea and let loose a massive beam of energy.

*Bang!*

Sorcea fell from the air again and Crystal marched toward her faster.

Scrambling, Sorcea rolled out of the way of a destructive beam shot at her. She gasped as she stumbled away, getting to her feet, and then suddenly flipping over a chair at the center of the floor. Around the room she ran, chanting with her eyes pressed on Crystal, dodging beams of energy as Crystal shot them.

"It will not be you who ends me," said Sorcea as she settled on the opposite side of the room. *'Avaros Macana,'* yelled Sorcea and twelve beasts made of water, fire, wind, and earth charged at Crystal at once.

"Parlor tricks," said Crystal and then rapidly as the beast neared her she spoke, *'Folo emm sa mistre.'* The beasts ran around her and turned to face Sorcea. They roared at once and rushed toward her faster than they had gone to attack Crystal.

"No!" At the top of her lungs she screamed and tried to flee. As she ran and levitated around the room, the beasts chased her. Each time she tried to utter Margortis, she could not finish the word.

One of the water beasts struck her and knocked her from the air, holding her in his watery guts. After fifteen seconds it fell to the floor, releasing her from its suffocating grip.

Halfway into a standing position an earth beast slammed into her, shattering on impact as it sent Sorcea careening into a window-wall.

*Clap!*

She fell to the floor and a fire beast was upon her, setting her on fire. Just before the fire began to bake her skin, she was swept up into a vortex by a wind beast, sweeping the fire away. It spun at forty-miles per hour and shot her out, onto the floor.

Sorcea was in agonizing pain and she let out a scream that rivaled her pain. Her palms were pressed against the floor as she tried to push herself up.

"I see that your will is not yet broken," said Crystal, with one eyebrow raised as if she were trying to find an answer to a question. *'Faanis nach,'* she uttered and another wave of attacks began.

"Please, no!" As *no* slipped from her lips, Sorcea was swept up into another vortex and spat out against the floor again. The fire beast engulfed her and then earth knocked her into the air, and as she flew she was doused and nearly drowned by the water a beast again. As she hit the floor, she panted, trying to suck in as much oxygen as she could.

Twice more the process occured and Sorcea lay on her back, bruised and bleeding from the pounding of the spell. Crystal stood over her, black eyes boring into her.

"Do you have any final requests that you'd like to make?" The look on Crystal's face was stern and unforgiving. No longer were her features soft and inviting. Her face held the expression of an unsatisfied hungry lion savoring the moment of its prey's defeat. Soon she would pounce to strike the final blow; the one that would leave no doubt that death had gripped her. Then complete satisfaction would come.

As her aura slipped from around her, it crawled toward her right shoulder. Strolling down her arm it hummed and as it reached her forearm it began to form a double-edged blade of energy. It stopped at a razor sharp point eight inches from Crystal's fist.

Touching the energy blade to Sorcea's stomach, Crystal watched her quiver in fear, trying to reach up and touch the blade of energy. But the sorceress was spent. She had no energy left to put up a fight.

"I think this is the exact spot." A deep frown creased Crystal's face. And she clinched her fist tighter, locking her black eyes onto Sorcea's. She watched her cower at her gaze and found pleasure it in. Sorcea's face screamed for her to stop, but she spoke no such request. "A life for a life." And as she flinched to press the energy blade into her enemy, a hand wrapped around her ankle. The familiar voice was nearly a whisper, but she heard it clearly.

"Have mercy. You are still a child. Don't become a killer. Have mercy, for me, have mercy on this one." Tears were running down Ms. Clark's face and Crystal looked at her stunned, and she grew angrier. "Be angry with me, but please have mercy." Her voice cracked and her body shook violently as she held her wound with her other hand, holding back the pain by force of will.

"Why?" The question was full of rage, rising like a crescendo, cracking the first layer of the window-walls.

"Because she is my sister." And her hand fell from Crystal's ankle as her face touched softly against the floor.

Crystal released a thunderous scream and all of her vengeful emotion surged and the energy blade raced into her chest, and she screamed louder. She watched Ms. Clark lift her head slowly as her eyes met with Sorcea. Seeing a tear run down Sorcea's face reminded her of her family. Crystal thought to herself that family you forgive, no matter the injury. In a flash, the black left Crystal's eyes, and tears raced from her eyes and she fell to her knees, her arms dangling limply by her sides.

As her head rolled down into her chest, she cried and again she sounded like a child. Her emotions overwhelmed her more as Ms. Clark's hand touched her knee. Never did she ever think that she'd see the little woman defeated. She had been too fierce to be taken down, but the truth of it was apparent.

Sorcea stared at Ms. Clark and Crystal caught her eye and she frowned at the sorceress, but did not move to attack her. Ms. Clark felt Crystal's rage surge and smiled at her sister softly and spoke the word, 'Magortis,' with an outstretched hand. The two of them watched Sorcea vanish from their sight, as Ms. Clark's hand slapped the floor, the last of her energy gone with the spell.

Crystal cradled Ms. Clark in her arms as she cried. The small woman looked at her with a smile. Crystal could still feel her pain, but it was suppressed by Ms. Clark's happiness. "Thank you." Ms. Clark had forced the words out, but they stabbed Crystal like a knife to the heart.

Harder she cried as she watched Ms. Clark inhale deeply and exhale her last breath, her eyes closing as she died in the arms of a child.

# OUT OF THE DEPTHS

The Danger Kids hung from the walls of Dorigon's throne room as he sat upon his throne with a focused scowl. Ray's hammer leaned against the arm of Dorigon's throne, and the Lord of Atlantis tickled the head of the hammer with his fingers. As he sat there he chanted in Atlantian and the entire chamber shook. Out of the windows, nothing could be seen except the blackness of the deep ocean. The sea creatures had long begun to flit away as the massive earthquake began.

Dorigon's dark eyes glowed as his stare was fixed on a point on the floor. His focus was unstirred as the Danger Kids struggled at their chains. They had tried for more than an hour to free themselves, but none of their powers worked. Long had they been told that their efforts would be futile but none of them listened. At least not until Dorigon's enchantments began to draw from their energy to aid in his plan of raising Atlantis.

Half of the city of Atlantis that hand sunken into the sea floor had already broken apart and the city had already begun to rise. Dorigon hadn't ceased his chanting since he began. He'd told them that he would raise the city to replace their home, but none of them truly believed him. But the city had once been there, sunken by Mysticgo long ago.

The very power that fueled their crests was the reason Dorigon had been forced to live under the tides of the ocean for so long. The very power that fueled their crests was the reason he had become frozen in time, seemingly never to rise again. Today the Danger Kids' power would bring Atlantis back to where it belonged. Out of the depths of the oceans, Atlantis would rise to the surface of the Earth, to replace New Covenant and become Dorigon's seat of power for all time.

Another hour went by as Dorigon chanted and the Danger Kids found themselves weakening more and more. Alex wondered if they should have taken his offer. All he really wanted to do was be a kid, graduate, and go to the dance with anyone who would say yes. He knew Kareem wanted the same things and Crystal, the girl he was too afraid to talk to.

There was a loud cracking and slowly the city began to float. "Ah," muttered Dorigon softly and raised his eyes from the point on the floor that he'd been watching. Standing, he felt the city rumbling slowly through the ocean and smiled. "It wont be long now." The smile on his face was filled with pleasure. He glided his hand across the top of Ray's hammer as he stepped down from the dais his throne sat upon. "Know that it is because of you that I have been able to do this thing. Therefore, I shall allow you to witness the destruction of your home before I end you."

"No thanks, kill me now," said Kareem rolling his eyes.

"You are yet too young to appreciate how momentous this occasion is. The whole of Earth will bow to me. The very eyes that stare at me with scorn will witness the changing of history. Should you not have such a grand story to speak about in the afterlife boy?"

"Yeah right, even if he was dead he wouldn't talk about you," said Aaron. "He's so full of himself that it's sickening some time. No offense." Aaron offered his last words lightly to Kareem.

"None taken, it's true," said a smiling Kareem.

*Boom!*

A ball of energy struck Kareem in the gut and knocked the wind out of him. He gasped so hard that he barely made a sound as his face wrinkled in anger and pain.

"Do you feel good about picking on children?" Mirely's eyes were filled with hatred for Dorigon.

"The last time I attempted to take the Earth, it was a group of children with your very powers that forced my hand to failure." Dorigon began circling the room as he spoke, with one hand behind his back. "I am comforted today in knowing that the lot of you are not nearly as practiced as your predecessors. And Mystic was nothing like her great ancestor. If he had not been such a generous fool, loving everything, he could have taken the world for himself. I was truly never a match for him. Not until he siphoned off his might to that lot of brats. That was long after the fight with his daughter. He'd never been the same after she died." Dorigon thought quietly for a quick moment, remembering days many years ago until Alex spoke.

"It was his daughter?" The revelation shocked Alex and the other Danger Kids as they began to mutter things between themselves.

"So your teacher told you of the story."

"She did, it was pretty good," said Anthony with a big smile on his face, remembering how much he enjoyed it.

"Shut up dweeb," said Aaron shaking his head annoyed.

Ray looked at Mirely and then his eyes darted to both sides and then lay back upon Mirely. "Mirely, your cousin," he began speaking to her, but she didn't respond. Surprise was still impressed upon her face as he said her name, "Crystal, where is she-"

"Yes the girl with the black eyes of Gandra," said Dorigon harshly in his guttural tone. "How I can't wait to watch her die."

"No," muttered Mirely, thinking about the story she'd heard from Ms. Clark.

Dorigon smiled at Mirely who was visibly shaken. "Too much power corrupts."

"Speak for yourself," she shot back.

Dorigon chuckled as he stared at her angry face. The tears streaming down her cheeks did not move him. He stood motionless, shaken only by the vibrations of his prized city moving toward the surface.

"We've got to get out of here," said Alex softly to Kareem.

Kareem looked at him with a defeated expression "How do you propose we do that?" He lifted his chains as high as he could, feeling terribly weak. "I can barely wiggle my fingers."

"Do you want to die hanging on a wall?"

The question was rhetorical, but Kareem answered it any way. "What do you think?"

"Then help me think."

"Do you realize how ridiculous you sound? I cheat off of your papers remember?" Kareem rolled his eyes and turned away from Alex. He couldn't believe he'd said that.

Meanwhile, Anthony hung relaxed in his chains whistling, looking around aimlessly at the room. He wondered what his friends were thinking. Mirely's tears had tugged at his heart, but he decided not to worry. "Hey mister, do you think we could have a bite to eat." He realized he'd been hungry for some time now. His belly growled at him twice.

"Are you serious?" asked Aaron, his voice nearly screeching.

"What?"

"I could eat myself," said Ray coming to Anthony's defense.

"Soon you'll all care nothing for food. And my dear Dark Shadow," began Dorigon and turned his eyes toward Alex, "you will not free yourself from my grasp."

"I knew he could hear us," barked Kareem at Alex.

*Swoosh!*

Through a portal came Sorcea landing hard and then skidding across the floor. Her hand slapped hard against the floor beneath her, bringing her body to a sudden stop. She gasped in pain, rolling onto her back.

Dorigon inclined his head in her direction and walked toward her slowly. On her face he could see bruises and cuts. She was clearly in pain as she struggled to her knees, bowing to him. One hand clutched at her belly and she panted as her king came to stand over her.

Touching her chin softly with two fingers he commanded her to look at him. Tears welled in her eyes, revealing an unspoken fear, as she watched him study her face. Her heart pounded in her chest as his lips began to move.

*'Odi shing faei emm?'*

Sorcea shook her head no.

*'Mystic sep's dusive've?'*

"Their teacher is gone to the afterlife," said Sorcea weakly. She knew Dorigon hated for her to commune with him in English, but she wanted the Danger Kids to know that Mystic was dead. She took some satisfaction in hearing their weeping as their shocked eyes ran with tears.

*'Wi aerr os belayst?'* asked Dorigon of the wounds. He remembered her having the upper hand on Mystic.

*'Lu gael heit l'ireis amordel emmi Ka,'* said Sorcea, referring to Crystal as the girl with the eyes of death. She believed that those eyes would be the last things she saw. If it had not been for her sister's mercy, she would have joined Mystic in the afterlife.

She wept as she dropped her head. How she took satisfaction from her sister's death, she knew well. She'd never been the apple of her parents' eyes. It had always been Mystic. That had been the reason she'd killed them so many years ago. Killing her sister proved to her that she was better. She proved her loyalty to her king. While Dorigon was cruel and even spiteful, she at least had felt appreciated whenever she succeeded. With him, as fearful as he made her feel, he accepted her as she was. In some strange way, it made her happy.

But now, deep in her heart, she regretted the action. Mystic had never been her enemy. Even at her worst, she loved her. At times she'd stand between Sorcea and her parents. Yet, constantly being compared to Mystic, only made her loathe her more over time.

*'Leyi sha al fae'l,'* said Dorigon, promising her that all the Danger Kids would all fall. He believed she wept for revenge, rather than regret. With her defeat of Mystic, he offered her a rare comfort. He pressed a glowing hand to Sorcea's face. The energy rushed through her and healed her wounds. Her energy had returned to her, and then Dorigon offered her his open hands. She placed her hands in his awaiting palms and he pulled her to her feet. Wrapping her tightly in his arms he hugged her tightly.

Sorcea was shocked at his display of affection. He had always seemed so cold and calculating, devoid of the most remote kindness. She thought that he might have been aware of her regret. He knew before he'd given her the order to kill Mystic that she was all the family she had. Could the King of Atlantis be so kind? Probably not, but she basked in the shelter of his embrace.

*Swoosh!*

Suddenly another portal opened and Crystal shot through with a scowl on her face. In front of her, the large old book that she'd seen Ms. Clark reading floated in the air. Looking around, she saw her friends chained to the wall, and felt the room vibrating under her feet.

Sorcea gasped at the sight of Crystal as she and Dorigon turned to see what had entered the room. Sorcea could see a smile on his face as he eyed the angry girl. She wished she could muster the will to stand before the girl confidently, but their last encounter destroyed any hope for it.

"Crystal!" Mirely screamed happily, tears still wet on her cheeks as the boys cheered her cousin's arrival.

With a flick of her wrist, Crystal release of bolt of energy from her palm. It moved too fast for the naked eye to see, and rammed into Dorigon's chest.

"Uh." Dorigon grunted as he hit the floor from the impact of Crystal's attack.

Sorcea crouched slightly, hands swirling with energy, as she stood at the ready, awaiting Crystal's next move. Fear gripped her tighter than it ever had before. Each encounter with the girl had found her beaten and fleeing. But in front of her king, in front of the Danger Kids, she could not flee.

"I spared you out of respect for Ms. Clark, because she begged me not to kill her sister. I will not be so kind now." Crystal's black eyes, tear less and unmoving allowed Sorcea nothing to read in her words, yet her grimaced face told the whole of her threat. It was a promise that she'd uphold.

Dorigon stood and laughed heartily, calling Sorcea to him. He whispered to her. "*Ogi nach ta lu kambri ayn odupref, tis odoji vo emm.*" His eyes glowed and a beam of energy connected to Sorcea's eyes. In that moment he imprinted an image in her mind with instructions of what she was to do. '*Nach!*' Barking at her in Atlantian, she spoke the spell and disappeared from the room.

"I'll give you the same chance I gave your friend. Surrender now or face your end," said Crystal, her voice deep and commanding.

"Your teacher tried to shield you from this doom. Your power is not great enough to subdue me. Like Gandra before, you shall try to summon power far greater than you can control. In that moment you shall die by my hand. And I shall give you a resting place; deep, dark, and cold as the winter's wind. This I pledge to you."

Dorigon strode toward Crystal, eying her and the book floating about near her.

Crystal noticed that he watched the book and smiled. "Scared."

"Ha," he yelled, "Mystic weaned nothing useful from that book in my wake. Sorcea offered her a quick death. I would have made her suffer, as I shall make you suffer now."

"Get him Crystal!" Kareem screamed and the others followed.

"The futile cheers of the doomed," said Dorigon as he shot toward Crystal, punching her square in the chest.

Crystal gasped as the force of the blow knocked her into the floor hard. She scrambled to her feet and found nothing in front of her.

*Bang.*

A boot struck her in the back and sent her flying forward, her hands pushing behind her.

*Clap.*

Suddenly she found her arms in Dorigon's grasp. "Did you think this would be pleasant?"

*Whoosh.*

His hands alit with energy and powerful kinetic energy shot through Crystal's body from the sides, knocking her to the floor on her back.

Dorigon's feet touched softly to the floor as Crystal stood slowly and craned her neck to one side. She touched the back of her neck and craned it to the other side and breathed in hard through her nose.

Nodding her head up and down, she smiled pleased at the circumstance. "A slight challenge," she said and began to laugh, cracking her neck from side to side. "This should be fun."

And in that statement, anger well up inside of the Atlantian king and he swung at her again. This time her fist met his own and a wave of energy surged between them, knocking them both back.

# INTO THE DARKNESS

The once pristine throne that Dorigon sat upon split in half. One side of it had fallen to the floor, broken into at least a half dozen pieces. The hard floor was cracked in several places as Crystal's back had landed into it. The glass walls were blemished with thin scratches, some as long as a foot. Most of the fixtures on the wall had shattered against the floor within the first minute of their contest.

The Danger Kids cheered Crystal on as she faced the King of Atlantis. They applauded the slightest advantage she could gain, but they were few and far between. As the fight wore on toward its twentieth minute, the Danger Kids found themselves cringing and screaming *oh*.

Crystal's lips were fat and red with blood after Dorigon's fist had found a home across her face. Her hair was half a fright, and her pants had ripped in two places. Yet, she stood before him with balled fists with an angry scowl, awaiting his next move. Her hands were surrounded by reverberating energy and her eyes remained as black as the night's sky.

Dorigon studied her for a moment, his face an unscathed mask of evil perfection. His eyes were intent on this child of an enemy before him, and soon he would pounce again. But something gave him pause to step slowly, and then turn and pace with a comfortable distance between the two of them.

Looking at the old book on the floor to his far left he begged a question of Crystal. "What is the spell you were hoping to perform when you bought that old ragged book?"

"One to rid the world of you," fired Crystal, spitting a glob of blood from her mouth onto the floor.

"So why not speak the words and be done with it?" he asked with a smile.

"Because you must be subdued first."

"You seem to be having some trouble with that."

"I kind of noticed."

"Get him Crystal!" Kareem shouted at the top of his lungs unable to stand the anticipation of when the next blow would be struck.

Crystal peeked up at Kareem and smiled softly. Uncertainty clouded her judgment. Up until now she'd fought back the urge to allow the gem to take over. With each blow, the gem's energy begged her to allow it to surge, to push itself further outward. But more than in herself, she believed in the story Ms. Clark had told. If she pushed too hard she'd bring about the destruction of Earth, herself, or both. That means her friends might die too. She didn't want to risk it.

Then something occurred to her, even in her haggardly beaten state. "Why have you been holding back?" The question caused Dorigon's brow to furrow as he leaned forward and pursed his lips in anger.

He then stood up straight and smiled, stopping his aimless march to give Crystal his full attention. "I would not if you would not." His tone was cool but filled with contempt. "I was there when Gandra's gem gave her the power to rival her father's own. You child have not given me the proper motivation to show you a fury that will make the world quake. And when I have grown bored with you, I shall separate your head from your body."

His threat was honest and chilling. Mirely felt the cold of it climb up her spine. "Beat him Crystal, save the world from him," she bellowed with tears in her eyes.

Cheers and exultations of hope and encouragement spewed from the lips of every Danger Kid. They believed she could beat him. They being chained knew she was their only hope to do so.

"You are not Gandra. You can control this thing," yelled Alex loudly. His voice was filled with pride and sincerity.

"Come on!" screamed Aaron kicking and flailing his limbs as much as he could.

"Yes, come now," said Dorigon turning his shoulders forward and stepping coolly toward Crystal.

The story Ms. Clark had told her played over in her head a dozen times as she stood there tense with balled fists. "It does not belong here," she remembered Ms. Clark saying. The power was from a hundred worlds away and it destroyed Gandra. "Never use this power again," Ms. Clark had also said. Mysticgo thought he'd die standing against his own daughter.

"Either way Earth is doomed." Crystal said quietly to herself. If Dorigon won, he'd make everyone slave to his rule. He'd sit upon his throne unopposed. Other than herself and the Danger Kids, no one else had come to stand against Sorcea and Dorigon. The police were put down in short order and all the people who weren't trapped in agony on the ground in front of City Hall fled to the safety of their homes. "Their homes wont be safe," she said, trying to motivate herself to act. "I'd rather die than be a slave because even in death there is freedom."

She decided that if the end of Earth was inevitable, then it should be by her hand. By her hand her friends would die and in her sacrifice not a single member of humanity would live under the guise of Dorigon. And she mocked him with the fury and passion of her anger. "You are an underwater king," she said, forcing back the lump in her throat so she would not cry.

Dorigon's scowl contorted his face and an anger that she hadn't seen in him before rose. An aura reverberated around his body and he rocketed toward her. The sound wave produced by the force of his movement splintered the floor and glass walls deeper.

Crystal could feel the surge of power that was the result of Dorigon's anger and the crystal gem around her neck danced softly. His fist slammed into her chest sending her careening backward. Her back banged against a pillar, and she fell to one knee.

The gem around her neck danced again and she smiled. The want to inflict pain and hear the screams of anyone near filled Crystal's heart and mind. She giggled as she stood and her eyes grew darker and the black light pushed out into the great throne room.

As it approached Dorigon he spoke *'Doru lu cacad."* With his hands he cut through the black light filling the room, and made his way toward Crystal. He could hear the Danger Kids scream as the light touched them.

Crystal felt their agony and basked in their wailing. Standing fast, she launched toward Dorigon and floored him with two quick punches to the face.

Kicking himself into a standing position he suddenly felt his legs kicked from under him. As he began to fall backward, a wave of energy hammered into his chest, knocking him into his throne.

Another piece of the broken throne fell to the floor. He bared his teeth at Crystal as she approached him slowly. Grabbing Ray's hammer, he catapulted toward Crystal and swung the hammer at her.

Ducking swiftly, she avoided the first blow and turned quickly to her right and punched Dorigon in his side. The blow barely moved him, as a field of energy seemed to push against her fist.

Swinging Ray's hammer again, Crystal jumped to the side and somersaulted forward as the hammer's head cracked the floor where she was standing. As she landed, she could hear the hammer howling in the air, ready to crash into her face. Slipping under, she allowed the hammer to sail above her and crash into a pillar.

Standing up straight, she found Dorigon's hands wrapped tightly around her throat. Suffocating, the gem around her neck pressed itself against her chest and the black light rushed out again, pushing Dorigon off of her.

"No not again," yelled Kareem as the light grabbed at him and the other Danger Kids, with more force.

"Crap," gurgled Anthony as he tried to rush from his chains with two futile attempts.

Mirely and Aaron wailed in agony, while Alex gnashed about in every direction hoping to free himself some way. The voice in his head returned again, mocking him, calling him weak, and he cried wet tears as his heart pounded in his chest. Ray was the only one who seemed to be able to withstand the stabbing grip of Crystal's black light. But the light gripped them again with more ferocity and they all bellowed their suffering.

"More," yelled Crystal and a sucking sound began and the light began to retract back into the crystal. Dorigon noticed that her eyes became blacker as she took the black light back into the gem.

Dorigon's eyes grew darker too, the burgundy of his eyes beginning to become black. *'Raagi de Minerva,'* he yelled and a shrieking scream entered the room and suddenly three ghastly witch spirits spewed from his mouth. One held a knife, one a spear, and the last a sword. They rushed toward Crystal through the air, swinging wildly with their weapons and clawing with their hands.

The screams of their voices, assaulted her ears, forcing her to turn her head to one side, and to close her left eye. The pain was intense and the spirit sword cut her across the shoulder. The wound seared as if burned and the witch's spear jammed into the wound the sword had made.

Crystal's back then seared as the third spirit whipped around behind her as she tried to avoid the cuts and stabs from the others. The squishing sound was unwelcomed and horrible as she felt the blade of the knife enter in and out of her flesh.

"Uh," Crystal yelled dropping to one knee. *'Sacessa,'* she screamed, expecting the witches to stop, but they only became more enraged, slicing and prodding faster at her flesh.

"Do you think those rudimentary spells will work against my magic?" Dorigon was boastful now, back to striding confidently as the Rage of Minerva curse worked Crystal to the floor. "Sorcea's power is nothing compared to my own!" He yelled his truth and raised his hands above his head at once.

A mass of energy formed between his hands, circling into a ball. When he threw it at Crystal the mass of energy chanted as it approached her. The witch spirits fled as the red ball of energy approached Crystal and disappeared.

Raising her arms in defense, Crystal turned away and felt the ball touch her. Her skin began to feel as if it were being assaulted by a million prickling needles and then the energy burst out. Each point where she felt her skin being pricked was hit with an electric shock.

Crystal shot backward on the floor, until coming to a bone-shattering stop. Her cheek slammed against the floor and she muttered in pain.

*'Harc de pye, emmon de freis,'* said Dorigon and a black shadow floated from his fingers like a black smoke and covered Crystal like a blanket. An ugly ragged voice, breathy and wicked spoke to her in a whisper.

The shadow lifted her body and she convulsed, floating into the air. All of her unspoken fears seemed to be right in front of her eyes and her confidence was shaken. Crystal kicked and screamed saying *no* all the while, wanting it to stop. She'd lost her composure and her eyes seemed to control her mind. Ugly rats, falling from a rollercoaster, her body being smashed in between two cars, and Brick carrying her over a threshold while she wore a wedding dress flashed across her vision. More and more fears erupted in front of her, and she nearly lost herself until she spoke a single word.

"Help." Her voice quivered and shook as she spoke and the gem pressed itself harder into her chest. All of the black light inside the throne room returned to the gem and the gem began to seep into her skin. Her skin became dotted with black marks and her costume returned to perfect condition. The bruises on her face were healed and the shadow that had wrapped itself around her, and nearly caused a psychotic episode retreated from her back into Dorigon.

When her eyes opened, a black beam of light all around her body shot up and out of the throne room, through the city, past the surface of the ocean and up into the sky. She could see it moving faster than she'd ever seen anything move before.

Slowly her body turned upright and the entire city began to shake as if an earthquake had struck it. The Danger Kids ceased to feel pain and the black light only wrapped itself around Crystal.

There was a booming sound in her ears and she felt a jolt when the black beam of energy had ceased to move. She looked up and knew that the beam was well out of the Earth's atmosphere and had collided with something a hundred worlds a way. She could feel a massive force filling her with energy.

Dorigon watched with his mouth hanging open. Alex looked at him and saw the first line of fear crease his face. Kareem looked at Alex with a sullen expression and blinked rapidly. "I don't want to die."

"I don't think we have much of a choice," said Alex as he watched Crystal descend to the floor and tilt her head from one side to the other.

"Crystal," said Mirely fearfully as she looked down upon her cousin. When Crystal turned her black eyes to her, she knew her cousin was long gone. A thin sheen of white covered Crystal's black eyes as she rolled them at Mirely.

"I wanted to ask you to the dance. If I would have asked you would you have gone with me?" asked Ray looking at Mirely, wearing his heart on his eyes.

"If you ask me I'll go with you," said Mirely with a weak smile.

"Will you go to the dance with me?"

"Yes," she said and cried happy tears.

Looking at his friends having their heartfelt moments as they faced their end, Aaron looked at Anthony. He rolled his eyes as the happy go lucky boy beside him shrugged his shoulders and curled his lips as if to says *whatever.* It bugged Aaron that Anthony wasn't afraid. He stared at him as the smallest of them looked on with eager eyes.

Anthony noticed that Aaron's eyes were still on him. "Everyone's gotta go sometime. At least we get to do it in style."

Aaron gave Anthony a defeated look chucked full of confusion and aggravation. But suddenly, the revelations of the boy's words changed into logic in his mind and he burst out in hearty laughter. "I guess dying next to you won't be so bad."

"Nope, we got front row seats to the end of the world," said Anthony winking his eye.

Dorigon saw the memory of his master and his daughter before him as he looked at Crystal. He looked at her as if he were staring at a ghost. Gandra was much older than Crystal, but she was still young. Her face had held the same innocence that Crystal's did, but the scowl on Gandra's face was there on Crystal's. Anger, rage, and retribution were etched into the lines of her expression. Her head rolled around as if she were in a trance and he saw her body jerking slightly from side to side.

The black beam of light surged from wherever it had connected into her, constantly filling her with energy. The black dots on her arms began to stretch out and connect to one another and began to form designs on her exposed skin. Around her eyes, tracking back to ears were markings that seemed to be words. Dorigon had never seen them and could not decipher them no matter how hard he tried.

"You'll not be the end of me girl," said Dorigon in a ravenous scream. "Feel my wrath!"

Rising into the air, Dorigon stretched his arms out wide. The broken pieces of throne and floor began to rise from the floor with the chips that had shattered below his feet. The throne room filled with a cold swirling air as Dorigon chanted in Atlantian, staring harshly at Crystal who simply stood, watching and waiting for what he'd do.

*'Freis de lue aganas!'*

A sound like a raging hurricane roared in the room and ten thousand spirits began swirling around the room. Bolts of lightning raged from Dorigon's hands. Fire belted from his mouth. With his ten thousand angry spirits of warriors and armed women, he made his way toward Crystal.

She watched him as he flew toward her with balled fists, blowing fire from his mouth. "Fright of the ages," she said repeating his Atlantian phrase. In that breath she understood his spell and what it would do. "Tears of the Mother." As she spoke, the black markings on her face, rushed into her eyes and out.

A wave of black energy shot out of her eyes and struck Dorigon with the force that shattered the glass windows around the throne room. The chains holding the Danger Kids in place shattered as the shockwave of black energy cascaded out into the room. The ten thousands spirits vanished from sight as Dorigon fell to his face on the floor.

Pressing his hands into the floor, Dorigon tried to push himself up, but collapsed back onto the floor. He rolled over onto his back and revealed a body of bruises and gashes as if he had fallen from a mountain. He was nearly spent. He panted quickly and his dark burgundy eyes began to brighten.

Crystal stood over him and looked down upon him with fury in her eyes. "You did not die," she said.

"Neither have you," replied Dorigon watching in shock as the black beams of energy that had struck him down began to pour back into her eyes, lining her face with markings again.

Ray pulled at his hammer and it slid loudly against the floor.

Crystal looked toward him fast and he put his hands up as if being commanded by a cop to freeze. "We're on the same team." Ray smiled and looked around at the rest of the Danger Kids, who were walking slowly toward Crystal.

Mirely held the book that had come through the portal with Crystal to her chest. "It's me cousin. It's us."

Crystal stared at them all for a moment with dark black eyes covered by a white sheen. Their faces she could not recognize, but their voices were familiar. "Cousin," she said almost as if asking a question.

"Friends," said Alex moving closer to her, reaching toward her.

She could read his mind and knew that he meant to touch her. Lifting her hand and yanking at his she pulled him closer and entered deep into his mind, seeing herself with him, Mirely, and then them all together with Ms. Clark smiling and laughing. "Friends," she said shaking her head *yes*.

The white sheen over her black eyes disappeared and her eyes slowly returned to their normal brown.

Suddenly she heard movement below her and then heard Ray's hammer swing, crashing into his chest. "Not so fast." Ray waved a finger at him.

"I know a spell to rid the world of him," said Crystal, looking happily at Mirely.

"Then say it and get rid of him," said Aaron with an arm around Anthony's shoulder.

"I'll be more than happy to listen to you say it," said Kareem standing over Dorigon facing Crystal. His eyes gave away his feelings for her, but she didn't quite notice it.

Alex curled his lips into his mouth fighting back his laughter.

"The six of you must say it. Together." Taking the book from Mirely, Crystal opened the book to the appropriate page.

"No," barked Dorigon, as he remembered being put into a tomb to sleep for all of eternity.

"This one you'll find isn't so kind as the last," said Crystal with great pleasure.

Looking at the book, Mirely blinked hard and looked at Crystal. "What are those, hieroglyphics?"

"No it's Atlantian," said Crystal and then she began to read them in English so the Danger Kids could hear them and speak them. "Repeat after me," she said looking around at them all. And as she spoke they spoke and continued to chant a half dozen times after ward.

*Into the darkness,*
*Into the well,*
*Into the realm, where devils do dwell,*
*With eyes of fire and heart of ice,*
*For all of time,*
*Be gone from sight.*

A golden ball of energy formed above Dorigon as the Danger Kids chanted the words that Crystal had taught them. Quickly the ball of golden energy dropped toward him and enveloped him, compressing Dorigon. The energy folded him inside of the ball of energy and he screamed in pain and fear as it took him and sucked him in. The golden ball of energy compressed to the size of a small man's fist and bobbed there for a few seconds. Suddenly it shot up and out of the throne room and through Earth's atmosphere and was gone forever.

The Danger Kids stood there with Crystal and watched the beam of energy that had connected with something a hundred worlds away return to her. She spoke the words that Ms. Clark had taught her; '*Revesti ef'iagi*,' and the lines on her face began to retract to the center of her chest and the crystal gem that had been around her neck emerged and reformed. Most of the black lines had turned back into dots, but this time they did not leave her skin completely. They remained like little beauty marks here and there. "Guess I'll have to find someone else to explain this." Crystal closed her eyes and shook her head no.

"We'll all be here to help," said Mirely wrapping her arms around her cousin tightly.

"Let's get out of here," said Anthony happily.

"Makes sense to me."

*'Sacessa dusive've,'* said Crystal and the entire city of Atlantis ceased to float toward the surface. "Who's going to do the honors?"

"I shall," said Kareem raising his hand wearing a big smile. "*Margortis teleportis.*"

The Danger Kids vanished from the throne room in the city of Atlantis and it sank back into the depths of the ocean.

# THE MORNING AFTER

Alex's glasses lay above the old book that they'd read the *Daca Zose Raim* spell from. He'd finally stopped crying and allowed his eyes to roam aimlessly over the unfamiliar words. With his elbows pressed against Max's control panel, he turned the pages, hoping that there was a curse that could bring the dead back to life. His eyes were still glossy with welling tears as he replayed the scene of the pallbearers setting her casket on the winch system in the cemetery. As her casket was lowered, hundreds of students and dozens teachers wept.

He remembered seeing Sorcea there as the priest said his final words. The tear on her cheek angered him, but Crystal's grip on his wrist forced him to stand still. Looking into Crystal's dry eyes made him cry harder, because she was being strong for them all, as they all had cried on her shoulder and into her chest that day. She'd been there at the end, and she satisfied Ms. Clark's request of mercy for her sister.

Everyone there thought Ms. Clark had died after losing control of her car, and slamming into a tree. All of the other students thought the cause of her death were severe trauma to the brain. None of them knew that she'd fallen trying to prevent the conquest of Earth by an evil king, long removed from power. He wanted to tell them the truth. He wanted to tell them that they were saved in part by her sacrifice.

They thought that the first earthquake to shake New Covenant was the work of nature. The beam of light was just some unexplained phenomenon in space that scientist would eventually figure out. That's at least what the news had been reporting.

Kareem's hands squeezing his shoulders snapped him out of his daydream. "You okay buddy?"

"Not really." Alex turned slightly, but didn't want to face anyone. He wanted to continue staring at the Atlantian script in front of him. "I'm not sure where we go from here." Rubbing his head twice, he cracked his knuckles and then folded his hands under his chin.

"We go one. We graduate. But we go to the dance first."

"I can't think about a dance right now."

"That's because you can't dance." Kareem laughed as he took a seat next to Alex.

"Thanks."

"You probably don't even have a date do you."

"And you do?"

"Yeah, Crystal," said Kareem with a huge smile and a flutter of his eyebrows.

"No way!" Alex was elated at the news. "So you worked up the courage to ask her?"

"She told me I was going with her."

"So you were ordered."

"Not one of my finer moments in life, but I ain't complaining."

"I bet." Alex smiled nearly as wide as Kareem had been since the news came to light. He was happy that his friend would go to the dance with the girl of his dreams.

Turning to his left he could see Mirely standing over a seated Ray, talking to him with a big smile on her face, as he leaned on his fist with an interested smirk. A forced smile lined Alex's face as Mirely gave him a wiggled finger hello. She'd turned as if she could feel his eyes on her, wearing a huge smile. Ray peaked over and squinted and quickly turned his eyes back on Mirely who met his own, blushing as she rolled her eyes in a girlish way.

"Yeah, even Mirely has a date, who would have guessed," said Kareem impressed. He'd never seen her talk so much with a smile on her face.

"What are you chumps talking about?" said Aaron who'd strolled up on their blind side.

"Probably the dance," said Anthony who'd walked up behind Aaron, bouncing a paddleball.

"Wow, look who keeps on getting bright," said Kareem snapping his fingers and pointing at Anthony.

"Check this out," said Anthony as he flung the paddleball across the room, zipping across in a flash before it hit the wall, and back to the group. Twice more he did it, faster each time. Then he bounced the ball against the floor. "Check this." The smile on his face was huge as stood there waiting as the ball began to fall. Half way into the fall he darted toward it.

*Crack!* A bolt of lightning struck the ball, causing it to burst. "Pretty sweet right." Aaron rolled his eyes, turning his attention back to Alex and Kareem as Anthony stood by the scattered pieces of his ball.

Anthony strolled slowly back toward them with a defeated look. Alex clapped him on the side of the arm. "Sorry about the ball." He forced back the smile that was trying to break through his somber mood.

Pulling another ball from his pocket, Anthony began to bounce it up and down. "No biggy, I always keep a spare." A big smile took over his face.

"He's been at it all morning." Aaron rolled his eyes again. "Everyone got a date?" Alex hoped the inquisition would stop.

"Not everyone," said Kareem pointing to Alex.

"Really? Even dweeb central over there's got a date," said Aaron shocked. "I thought all the women loved you Elwood." Anthony shook his head *yes* as Alex and Kareem looked at him shocked.

"They do, they're teachers. I have a harder time with the girls." Alex breathed in and exhaled as if to say *whatever.*

Crystal swept into the room through a portal with three books in her hands. "Morning beautiful - beautiful's boyfriend," she said to Mirely and Ray dismissively as she walked swiftly toward Kareem.

"Thanks a lot." Mirely's cheeks flushed a darker red.

"Everyone already knows." Crystal yelled back as she continued to march toward the four boys at the control panel. "Hold these." Slamming her books into Kareem's arms, she watched as he fumbled to keep them up.

"Indentured servitude," said Alex to make a joke.

"Dude seriously, you need to brush up on your history." Kareem was fuming at Alex for his joke, but he wasn't going to put the books down to try and prove his manhood.

"We've one hour before school and we've got a few things to go over. Firstly, I don't take orders since I'm the only one who can read Atlantian. That spells is about how to make someone fall in love with you," she said pointing at the book. "I hear you only need a date." Swinging her hand in a sweeping motion, Crystal forced the book to close. "You all now write for the school paper. Ray you have Elmwood's job, and Kareem, you're my assistant."

"What?" Kareem was floored by the news.

"Who put you in charge?" asked Aaron confused.

"I did, I'm smarter than the rest of you."

"I can argue that," shot Alex.

"Mirely helps you, you don't do it alone Elmwood, so spare me. Not to mention you're never on time for anything." Crystal had barely paused to take a breath before she began to speak again. "So...we'll meet here every morning at seven to work on our skills and learn Atlantian. Any questions?"

Kareem raised his hand as high as he could, while he kept her books secured between his arms. "How long do I have to hold these?"

"Until we go to school," said Crystal incredulously. She laughed out loud and the rest of the group followed as Kareem made a wicked face. "No, you can put them down now." Crystal winked at Alex as Kareem turned quickly to put the books down and relieve himself of the weight.

"Are you really serious right now?" asked Anthony.

"No, but I had them all shook up right," said Crystal raising her hands to slap high fives with Anthony. He swung and nearly fell over. "Okay."

Then unexpectedly a voice entered into the hall that didn't belong to Max. It was deep and smooth. "So now there are seven Danger Kids."

"Who the," said Kareem standing and spinning around. Ray too had stood up and began to turn his head from side to side looking around the room.

"You hear that," said Ray looking down on Mirely.

She'd already stepped closer to him and grabbed hold of his shirt with one hand and then turned to stand by his side. Her fingers interlocked with his, as her heart began to pound.

A soft hissing sound entered the room and was followed by a flash of dark blue light. From the light came a tall man, two inches over six feet. His brown skin was flawless. He stood upright with broad shoulders, wearing fine embroidered dark blue robes, a black cape and tall black boots. Upon his waist he wore a sword and his left hand sat on the pommel of it, caressing a beautiful blue jewel.

"And who exactly might you be?" said Crystal feeling the gem around her neck vibrating.

"It seems your Black Moon Gem fragment knows quite well," said the handsome man, showing perfect white teeth.

Crystal touched her fingers to the gem around her neck. "You know what this is?" She looked at him in awe; happy to have heard the name of the gem she wore around her neck.

"Quite intimately. I knew the Chalendoran Mysticgo, who gave it to Gandra, his daughter; the girl who was killed by it's power. And I was sent by the god who gave it to him many moons ago as a gift to take with me the one who called out to him."

"Take her, I think not," said Ray transforming into Danger Kid form. He held his hammer at the ready and began marching toward Crystal and the stranger who had come, and pushed Crystal behind him.

Lifting his hand, the brown-faced stranger turned up his right palm and looked in his hand. He squeezed his hand shut and then opened it and Ray's crest sat in his palm, missing it's marking. Ray gasped as his armor, helmet, and hammer broke into a billion pieces, each the size of a grain of sand. He watched with his mouth wide as the tiny pieces zipped into his crest, forming the marking anew upon his crest.

"Whoa," said Anthony astonished.

Alex was stunned and they all began to back away from him.

"Who are you?" Kareem's voice was a girly whisper as he held his fingers to his mouth amazed.

The man smiled.

"I am Cornelius Farrell, from The Order of Halo Masters, and we have much to discuss before Crystal and I depart."

And the room fell to silence.

Here Ends The First Book
Of The Danger Kids
The Story Will Continue
In Book Two.

# MEET THE AUTHORS

*De'Quan Foster* was born on the 16th day of August in 1994. He began writing the Danger Kids series when he was eleven, on May 19, 2006. As a child, Foster was bullied and made fun of for his appearance and some of the interests he had. Some of those interests included the *Star Wars* films, *Marvel* and *DC* comics – their movie adaptations, and the *Harry Potter* book series. He drew inspiration from these interests and soon began developing the Danger Kids. *The Twelve* was his first published work. *A Generation's Journey* marks his second published work.

*A.S. Washington* was born on the 19th day of September in 1983. He graduated from Temple University with a degree in Economics, and lives in New Jersey where he works with at-risk teenagers. As a boy he fell in love with books and began writing his own stories. In December of 2011, his debut novel, *The Virgin Surgeon* was published. In the summer of 2012, his first collection of poetry, *The Musings of My Epic Mind* was published. *The Twelve* was his third published work. In the fall of 2013, A.S. Washington published Book One of the Weary King Series, *Words of the Weary King*, a collection of poetry. *A Generation's Journey* is his third novel and fifth published work.

For more on these authors and the Danger Kids Universe go to:

TWITTER.COM/MRDEFOSTER
TWITTER.COM/ASWASHINGTON